BALSAMIC MOON

BALSAMIC
MOON

ALAN GARTENHAUS

atmosphere press

For Rhoady.

With thanks to Susanna, Jackie, Susan, Cathy, M.P., J.O., Maureen, Mark, Marla, Lori, Tina, and Richard for their time, support, and encouragement.

DAY ONE
Friday, August 26

Opera thundered from inside the house next door. Doreen shook her head. Richard Girard played it constantly, and so loud. She didn't understand her odd reclusive neighbor, or his choice in music. She suspected that he might be unwell and wondered if he was eating right. *Men are no good at caring for themselves. Women know how to, for sure, but men? They aren't built like that.*

Climbing into her car, she saw Richard staring out his living room window, arms crossed over his chest. He looked upset. She raised her hand in a hesitant greeting. He might have smiled in response, she couldn't tell. He quickly disappeared behind curtains yanked closed.

She backed out of their shared driveway heading for the Winn-Dixie to stock up on supplies—bottled water, canned goods, candles. A hurricane had crossed south Florida and entered the Gulf. It was the season. She also needed to get dog food. She'd bought a yellow Lab for her son as a birthday surprise. Imagining Curtis' face when he returned from summer camp and saw the dog thrilled her.

On the drive, thoughts of her neighbor pushed forward. *I should make that man something to eat. Mama's shrimp stew. Everyone loves it.* Doreen wriggled in her seat, pleased with herself. *Doing the good work.* She turned onto Franklin Avenue and headed to Bayou Seafood.

DAY TWO

Saturday, August 27

He had the lightning dream again—the last flash so intense it struck him awake. Richard blinked hard, took two deep breaths, and reached for his eyeglasses, his fingers adding new smears to old smudges. It was only a few minutes past midnight; he hadn't slept long. His head returned to his sweat-stained, sour-smelling pillow. Stifling heat had continued for weeks without a single thunderstorm to break the cycle. No thunderstorms, no lightning. Richard craved lightning the way a junkie craves drugs. He ached for it—the thrill of it. Glorious white-hot flashes that affirmed his belief in a higher power and interrupted life's unending monotony. But lately, lightning only came to him in dreams, taunting him like an itch he couldn't reach—impossible to ignore, impossible to quell.

Knowing that sleep would not return, he stood and trudged into the bathroom, wincing when he flicked on the light and caught sight of his reflection in the medicine-chest mirror. Dark circles surrounded even darker eyes. He'd once been thought quite handsome. Everyone had said so. Leading-man material. But at age fifty-nine his features had coarsened, his sallow skin sagged, and his once thick, mahogany-colored hair had thinned, becoming brittle and gray.

After brushing his teeth and wrapping himself in the flimsy blue terry-cloth bathrobe that had been given to him by a friend he'd lost contact with years earlier, Richard shuffled through the empty house and into the dark kitchen without turning on the light, ignoring the clutter and unwashed dishes in the sink. He opened the refrigerator and smelled the milk. It had only just begun to spoil. He poured some into a small bowl and carried it to the back of the house where a scruffy white cat waited, depositing tufts of fur as she rubbed against the rusted screen door.

Richard turned on the outside light. "Hello, Blanche." His knees cracked when he bent down to stroke her. Rewarded by her purr, he smiled. *"Ma petite."* He cooed while scratching favorite spots behind her tattered ears. "Sweet little Blanche de la Rue." He set the bowl on the back step and watched as she lapped at it. Blanche had simply arrived one evening several years earlier; he'd fed her, and she'd remained, claiming for her own the open area under his house, which stood above the ground on brick pilings. Blanche defended her modest domain vigorously and had notches missing from her ears that proved it.

After returning the emptied bowl to the kitchen and setting it with others in the sink, Richard headed for his parents' bedroom. He often walked in there. He missed them immeasurably. He opened a gold-filigreed jewelry box that sat on his mother's bureau, removing her beaded rosary and coiling it in the palm of his hand. Though he'd long ago left a church that had rejected him, he made the sign of the cross and began to pray, calling upon St. Joseph, who had provided Mary and Jesus with shelter, to protect his modest home. A hurricane had entered the Gulf of Mexico. Its presence threatened his house and its contents, which were not simply the physical remnants of his life and that of his deceased parents; they were all he had left in this world.

Threading a path through his dimly lit living room, and ignoring old newspapers scattered on the carpeted floor, he passed his favorite high-backed chair, foregoing it to sit outside on the cooler concrete of the front stoop. The end of August in New Orleans guaranteed jungle heat and humidity, and time that moved more slowly than its thick moist air. Though his house lacked air conditioning, he rarely sought relief outdoors unless it was very late and sleep wouldn't come. He enjoyed marveling at those few stars bright enough to compete with the lights of the city but would only do so when he could linger unnoticed and undisturbed. Tonight, more stars shone than usual. They had less competition. The threat posed by an approaching hurricane had scattered wary neighbors like milkweed on a summer breeze.

Reports on the radio warned that the storm in the Gulf had grown in size and strength. Now more than 450 miles across and packing winds over 160 miles per hour, she was said to be pushing a surge of water twenty-five feet and more into the air. Comparisons were being made to Hurricane Andrew, which had destroyed every part of south Florida it touched, but with one important difference: this storm was far larger than Andrew.

Richard pictured the storm as a circular saw lying on its side, an enormous spinning blade approaching landfall. Though its precise route and landfall remained in question, all day a mocking little tune had played in his head. *The wind began to switch, the house to pitch, and suddenly the hinges started to unhitch.* His nightmare was being trapped in the house as it exploded, peppered and pierced by countless wooden slivers. But it wasn't death he feared most, it was survival—the dread of being left physically devastated and, far worse still, homeless. He had known little beyond these walls for years. And while his retreat and isolation had resulted in a life untended, a life of neglect and indifference, with mirrors that only reflected the past, it had also rooted him firmly in place. At least the discomforts here were familiar and predictable.

Surveying the other houses in his neighborhood, he saw that stragglers remained. Light flickered from Doreen's television next door. Although Fay and Nolan were in their home across the street, their car was already packed with boxes and a large canvas bag had been strapped to its roof. Richard assumed everyone would leave eventually, that he would soon be the only person left on the block.

Richard's thoughts were interrupted when the front light outside of the house next door turned on. His eyes narrowed. Doreen Williams's door opened and a large light-colored dog he had never seen before lumbered down her steps. He watched it waddle onto the grass and lift its leg. When the dog noticed Richard, it galumphed across the lawn, tail wagging and tongue hanging from the side of its mouth. Richard put down the cigarette he was about to light and reached out with both hands. "Who have we here?" The dog was obviously friendly and happy to make his acquaintance.

He heard Doreen whistle. A moment later, he saw her step outside onto her landing and call out, "Buddy!"

"He's over here," Richard replied. The hefty dog exhaled loudly while dropping down beside him.

Everything about Doreen jiggled, from her turquoise-colored housecoat cinched with a cloth belt, to her head full of pink sponge curlers. She crossed their narrow strip of adjoining lawn. "Already a troublemaker! Hope he isn't bothering you."

Richard shook his head. "I love dogs." His hand continued stroking the dog's broad back. He would have liked his neighbor to return inside and let the two of them have a little more time alone together.

Doreen's face beamed. "Gentle, huh? And mellow. Just got him. He's a surprise for Curtis. It's his eleventh birthday on the sixth. My boy has wanted a dog for as long as I can remember."

"Where is Curtis?"

"Sent him to a sports camp our church sponsors, up near the Arkansas border. He's supposed to come home Monday, but who knows—what with the storm and all."

"A sports camp? What sport does he play?"

"Oh, none yet. That's why I sent him. Wanted him to try them all out."

Buddy rolled onto his back. Richard rubbed his tummy. "This dog's no puppy."

"I know. He's seven. I bought him from some people in Metairie who couldn't keep him. I've never owned a dog before, so I wanted one that was already trained."

Richard nodded. "Welcome to Mandeville Street, Buddy." The dog stood and shook his entire body, his ears flapping against his head. He sauntered down Richard's four front steps and joined Doreen on the grass, where he settled, his legs splayed in different directions.

"What are you doing out here so late?" she asked, her hands reaching up to touch the curlers in her hair as though suddenly self-conscious.

"Can't sleep when it's hot like this."

She tightened the belt around her robe. "Hurricane's got me nervous." She gazed up at the sky. "Hard to believe it could be coming our way. It's such a clear, starry night."

Doreen leaned over and patted the dog's solid body. "I hate this not knowing, don't you?"

Richard hummed his agreement. "When are you leaving?"

She shook her head. "Don't think I will. Last year Curtis and I spent close to two hundred dollars on a hotel room in Lake Charles just to watch Ivan turn and hit Biloxi." She frowned and cocked her head to the side. "These damn storms always spin off at the last minute and hit someplace no one expects, don't they?"

He nodded thoughtfully while lighting a cigarette.

"I can't be spending that kind of money every time bad weather comes our way. And you've seen my rattle-bucket of a car." She pointed at her thirteen-year-old rusting Toyota Tercel and sighed with resignation. "What about you? What are you going to do?"

"Sit in my living room and listen to opera." Richard gazed skyward, made the sign of the cross, and clasped his hands as if in prayer. "But no one should take their cues from me. I'm sure the safest thing would be to get the hell out of here. Watch all the fun from a distance."

Doreen harrumphed. "I've already stocked up. Got plenty of food." Her curlers bounced. "And tomorrow I'm going to cook up a storm." She surprised herself with the unintended humor and laughed, high-pitched and spiraling. "Thought I'd fill some extra bottles with water and make a safety retreat in the bathroom. I'm planning on pulling blankets and clothes over me. I'll hide in the tub if things get too bad."

She met Richard's chuckle about her climbing into the bathtub with a nervous titter. "Come on, Buddy," she said and clapped her hands. "Time for bed. Your mama's beat." When the dog didn't move, she bent down and tugged at his collar. As they walked away, she wished Richard a good night's sleep.

Too agitated to sleep, Doreen dressed, shut Buddy in the bathroom with a big bowl of water, and drove to the French Quarter craving beignets—a guilty pleasure, especially during times of stress. Sitting at a small table in the Café Du Monde among raucous tourists stretching their late night into early morning, she ate, unaware that powdered sugar had fallen from the pillow-shaped doughnuts and trailed down the front of her blouse.

She congratulated herself on resisting the last few bites. She could easily have devoured every crumb, but had been gaining weight, and buying new clothes was expensive. When finished, she left the café and crossed Decatur Street, choosing to take a stroll around Jackson Square on her way back to her parked car, admiring the urban park and the Pontalba apartment building with its lacy iron galleries. She rarely got to enjoy the square's graceful, tiered fountains, iron fencing, and vibrant crape myrtles, especially when empty of its usual crowds. She paused before St. Louis Cathedral, its façade and three pointy spires lit up dramatically and looking beautiful. Built in the early 1700s, this was the oldest Catholic cathedral in continual use in the United States and, though she was not a Catholic, Doreen had long wanted to attend a Mass here and experience the spectacle. Together with the elegant Presbytère and Cabildo buildings that flanked either side of the Cathedral, these were among New Orleans' most important landmarks and some of the finest examples of French and Spanish colonial architecture anywhere.

As she stood, blotting perspiration from her bronze neck, wondering how the night could be so deathly still with such a ferocious storm churning in the Gulf, a thin female voice interrupted her quiet reflection. "Young lady. *Venez. Venez ici.*" Doreen turned. Tucked into a recess of Pirate Alley, a slight, elderly woman sat at a small folding table, motioning with both hands. Illuminated only by the alley's gas lamps and dressed in black, she had gone unnoticed, blending into the shadows. The woman wore large dark glasses, which Doreen assumed to be an affectation in the dim flickering lamplight. Her cardigan sweater seemed equally unnecessary in such sultry weather. Doreen strained to make out the words on the hand-lettered sign sitting atop the woman's table. *Tarot Readings with Mercy.*

Remembering once again that the theme of her last sisterhood meeting at church had been "doing the good work," she walked over and pushed a dollar bill into the old woman's glass jar.

"But I did not ask you for money," the woman protested as Doreen began to leave. "And now you walk away from me? Why? Does the idea of talking with me frighten you?"

Doreen squared her shoulders, spun around, and faced the woman. "Do I look scared?"

"I wouldn't know." The old lady removed her dark glasses, revealing eyes covered with whitish clouds. Her enlarged left eye turned at an odd angle. She picked up a white cane and pointed to a dog cloaked in a service harness and snoring softly at her feet. "I am blind. I see what others cannot."

Doreen bowed her head. "I'm sorry. But why, then, did you ask me over?"

"I sensed something about you. Heard it in your walk."

"Sensed what?" she asked.

"I'm not sure—a concern, a sadness, perhaps disappointment. I felt you had questions for the cards." The old woman's voice rattled a bit, as if she needed to clear her throat. "Have you? Have you questions?"

Doreen sighed with resignation as she dropped onto the small chair before her. She fanned her flushed face with her hand. She could see that the woman was quite old. "Can the cards tell me when this heat will break?"

The woman frowned. "Tarot does not predict the weather. I only know that with the approach of a balsamic moon something big is coming, but that wasn't your question, was it?" She held out a deck of dog-eared, oversized cards that appeared even larger in her tiny hands. "Shuffle them. Let me read them for you."

"Tarot Readings with Mercy." Doreen recited aloud the words on the woman's sign. "So, you color your readings with kindness?"

"Hardly." The old woman huffed, pulling her sweater more tightly around her narrow chest. "The cards are the cards. Mercy is my name. Actually, my true name is Merci. My mother lost three before me."

Doreen received the deck from Mercy's bent, knurled fingers. "But if you're blind, how can you see them?"

"You will shuffle and I will lay them out. Then I'll ask you to tell me about them. We will make this reading together."

Doreen attempted to return the cards after shuffling only once, but Mercy resisted. "*Non.* Take your time. Reflect as you shuffle. Think about where you are in life, and about the questions you have. You needn't say anything to me, but do shuffle the cards with intention. Place them next to your heart. Make them your own."

Even by such soft, romantic light, Doreen could see blood pumping through the vessels in Mercy's translucent forehead and cheeks, marked as they were with purple splotches. Age had etched deep creases in the woman's face, but her high cheekbones and delicate features suggested former beauty, and the several strands of gray in her dark hair glistened. After shuffling and caressing the cards and placing them against her chest, Doreen cradled Mercy's hands and gently returned the deck to her outstretched palms.

"Are the cards facing me as they did you?" the old woman asked.

Doreen took the deck and rotated them. "They are now."

"Bon." Mercy dealt the cards, snapping each one as she flicked it from the deck and set it onto the table. The first six she placed in the shape of a cross, the next four in a vertical line directly beside it, and the final twelve in a horizontal row below all the others. Some of the cards were right side up, others upside down. Once done, she wheezed and drew several labored breaths; it seemed the mere act of dealing had tired her. *"Un moment, s'il vous plait,"* she said, folding her hands as if in prayer. She then put her hands over her eyes. Moments later she leaned forward and whispered, "Your soul will be touched."

"My soul will be touched?" Doreen shook her head. "I don't understand. What does that mean?"

Mercy smiled slightly. "I don't know. It is the answer to one of your questions. Now hush." She removed her dark glasses and rubbed the sides of her nose with her index fingers before cupping her hands over her eyes and mumbling an incantation that sounded like gibberish. Finally, she lowered her hands and fell silent, shaking her head as if responding to silent voices. Even in such low light, Doreen could see that Mercy's complexion, which was the color of lightly toasted bread, had paled. "Perhaps we should not go further with this," she warned, her expression disturbed. "You will not welcome what these cards say."

"I thought you couldn't see."

"I cannot. But I do sense things."

Doreen scoffed, annoyed. "You've already gotten me to go this far."

"True." Mercy's countenance grew grave as she nodded slowly. "Tell me the six cards placed in the middle, if you would. Start with the two that touch one another."

Doreen looked down at the cards. "One is the Empress; the other's the Hermit."

"Ah, yes, and their directions?"

"Both are facing me, so I figure they must be—"

"Of course. They would be reversed."

"Okay. Reversed. Above them is the World. I guess it's also reversed. As is the Fool to the right and the Wheel of Fortune to the left. Only the Hanged Man at the bottom is not."

The old woman shuddered and shook her head. Taking a halting breath and moaning softly, she slumped forward. "But this is not good, not good at all. I knew it. I could feel it before you even told me about the cards. *Quelle tragédie.*"

Doreen leaned closer. "What's not good?"

Mercy exhaled. "*Écoutez.* It is for you to listen and decide for yourself. I do not know more than what the cards tell." Mercy's hand moved forward until it found Doreen's forearm. "It seems there is enormous sadness near you. It draws you. This sadness is due to the passing of an Empress, a female person of great influence. Someone held most dear."

Doreen's jaw clenched. Her mother, a diabetic, had been ill for quite some time, and her health had been failing lately.

Mercy squeezed Doreen's arm more firmly. "As for the surrounding influences, above this enormous loss is a card of material wealth. The World. But you've said that it, too, is in a negative position, which means such matters are in disharmony and will only get worse. Below all this is the Hanged Man, a card of sacrifice, indicating even more that must be given up."

"More? More of what? What would that be?"

Mercy hunched her narrow shoulders. "As I told you, I only know what the cards say. It is up to you to figure out what they mean."

"But how can I? I don't understand."

"All I do know is that it will be something precious."

Doreen immediately thought of her son and became alarmed.

"And the cards tell that this bad luck, these hard times, will not change," Mercy continued. "Things do not get better. No change of season. *Une honte. Plus de tristesse.* Things will be beyond your control. The bad fortune around you will not go away but will grow."

Doreen stood abruptly, nearly toppling the folding chair on which she sat. Both of her parents were elderly and fragile, and her young son was away from home for the first time at summer camp, with bad weather approaching. More of this talk would overwhelm the anxiety she'd already been carrying. "Thank you, Miss Mercy. It's late. I'd better be going."

"Forgive me," she implored. "I only read the cards. I do not make the future."

"No, of course not." Doreen took a five-dollar bill from her purse and folded it into Mercy's hand. "I must go. Good night."

As Doreen turned to leave, already working to dismiss everything she'd heard, Mercy called out, "Do not forget that a storm is on its way and a balsamic moon is coming as well. With cards like yours, you must take care. Be aware, my dear. Prepare. Watch out for the balsamic moon."

The sun rose on a new day. Doreen looked out her kitchen window, relieved. Calm skies. Hardly a cloud. She switched radio stations from news to music. Why not? After last night's tarot reading, listening to forecasters banter about the hurricane's path could only increase her apprehension. The weather outside was clear and tranquil. Why fret when storms always turn? She told herself to focus on the stew she was making. It required her immediate attention.

She turned up the volume on the radio. Aretha's exhilarating voice supercharged Doreen's spirit and added to her motivation. "R-E-S-P-E-C-T," she sang along, while increasing the heat under the cast-iron Dutch oven and dropping in chopped green bell peppers, onions, and celery—the New Orleans' holy trinity—stirring as they sizzled and popped in her darkening roux. Shrimp she'd peeled bobbed in a bath of icy cold water in the sink. Bay leaves, salt, and cayenne stood at the ready. Her mother's recipe. She knew it by heart; she'd made it a hundred times.

Markita surprised her, entering the kitchen undetected and calling out, "Hey good-lookin,' whatcha got cookin'?" loud enough to be heard above the blare of the radio. Doreen jumped and then hooted, laughing at herself. "Good Lord, girl, you nearly gave me heart failure!"

Doreen and Markita had been close friends their whole lives—and, as they were fond of saying, even before—their mothers having been good friends and pregnant with the two of them at the same time. The two women had gone through school together, and double-dated together. Doreen had been Markita's maid of honor. Markita had held Doreen's hand in the delivery room when she gave birth to Curtis. They taught at the same elementary school. They had gone through much of life's ups and downs together. They knew each other's secrets.

Markita's enthusiasm was reflected in her animated demeanor. "Did you hear? *Wheel of Fortune* taped a couple of shows down at the Convention Center on Friday."

"That so?" A tremor registered through Doreen's core as she turned the radio off. The Wheel of Fortune had been a significant card in her tarot reading with Mercy last night.

"Francine Delray told me that Pat and Vanna sat at one of her tables in Brennan's. Said they were nice. Left her a generous tip." Markita grabbed a hunk of French bread from Doreen's cutting board, stuck it on the end of a fork, and plunked it into the thick brown gravy. "Forgive me," she said as she swirled the bread around before blowing on it. "I can't resist." She popped it into her mouth.

Doreen drained the shrimp using an old colander she'd gotten from her mother years earlier and slid them into her well-seasoned cast-iron pot on top of the stove. She pushed them around as they turned from gray to bright pink. "So, what's up, sugar? Or did you just come over to tell me about *Wheel of Fortune*?"

Markita pointed at the heavy-set dog lying on a large pillow on the kitchen floor. "I came to see Buddy again." Doreen smiled as Markita walked over and gently stroked the sleeping dog's large head. Buddy awoke and wagged his tail, happy to have the attention. "Curtis is one lucky guy! You know he's going to go berserk."

"I don't want to talk about that boy." Doreen's hands went to her waist. "I'm annoyed with him. I gave him five stamped postcards, each one already addressed and ready to mail. He promised to write and let me know how he was doing. So far, I've only received two, and they both came the first week."

Markita chuckled and shook her head. "That's a good sign. It just means he's enjoying himself and isn't homesick." She looked at her friend. "So, is that all?"

"As a matter of fact, it isn't. A couple weeks ago, I asked Curtis to help Nolan Lagusi clean out his garage. Thought it would be good for him to learn about work and to earn a little money. Nolan promised to pay Curtis ten dollars. But he forgot to get paid and threw a fit when I told him to go back and ask for it. Flat-out refused. Said he wouldn't."

Markita curled her bottom lip into a pout. "Your boy's a shy guy. He was probably too embarrassed, don't you think?"

She raised her hands in the air. "Now they're telling me he won't be coming home until Wednesday, which seems like forever. It's all I could do not to call up there and tell him about the dog. Ruin his damn surprise."

Markita rubbed the dog's head, chuckling. "Wasn't he supposed to come home on Monday?" Buddy looked up at her as though he were smiling.

"Reverend Watson said he's keeping the kids upstate for an extra couple of days until the bad weather passes. They just called to tell me."

Markita hummed thoughtfully. "You know, it's not a bad idea. Plenty of folks are hightailing it out of here. Looks like Fay and Nolan are getting ready to go. Sam's been talking about leaving, too, maybe later this afternoon. He's glued to the news. His motto is why take chances?"

"How smart are you going to feel when that hurricane follows you to Galveston?" Doreen thought about how Markita had always preferred predictable men like Sam—comfortable sedans who were accommodating, safe, and easy to repair; whereas she had gone for guys more like sports cars—racy, temperamental, and exciting, but far more likely to break down on you. Then again, Markita and Sam had been married for ten years. Doreen's only long-term relationship had been with her son's biological father. And he had taken off when she announced her pregnancy, leaving her to raise their child on her own.

Markita ate a shrimp and rolled her eyes with delight. "So good. You freezing some? You do know all this shrimp stew won't keep till Wednesday." She glanced at Doreen for permission to take another bite. "You're making quite a lot."

"I'll be making more when Curtis gets back. This isn't for us. It's for Richard."

Markita set the fork down. Her eyebrows knitted. "Richard? Richard who?"

Doreen waved away her implication. "Richard. The man next door." She pointed toward her neighbor's home, which was nearly close enough to reach out her window and touch. "You know, he's the one that . . ."

"Oh, I know who *he* is all right." Markita physically stiffened. Her expression shifted to one that scolded. "What? Are you two friends now or something?"

"Not really. It's just that some of us women from church have been talking about getting more involved and helping out folks in need. You know, doing more of the good work. Being that he lives next door, I thought I should start with him."

"And you think dropping off a bowl of shrimp stew makes you some kind of a saint?" Markita hissed and shook her head. "You do know that man's crazy."

"All the more reason to help him out. Maybe the Lord will give me bonus points."

"Well, I think he's a pervert like that freaky guy in the movie *Psycho.* I've seen him peeking out his windows, watching the kids around here a little too close."

"You're wrong. He's quite the timid sort," Doreen said, frowning. "And harmless. Besides, I don't think he's well. The poor guy's looking thin and pale."

"He's white, Dory," Markita replied, a wry smile on her lips. "White folks always look pale."

Doreen laughed. "No, for true. I'll bet he doesn't have a thing to eat in that house. He doesn't look good."

"You're telling me! He doesn't look *right,* either. Honestly, don't you find him strange? I mean, what's with that music he plays all the time? You'd think he lived in a haunted house with all that's going on over there. And those things he wears on his ears! Makes him look like a mouse. What in God's name are they supposed to be?"

"They are something, aren't they?" Doreen clasped her hands and giggled. "He doesn't wear them all the time. And, so what if he did?" She shook her head. "I feel bad for him. Fay told me he's been extremely depressed since his mama died."

"Aha! You see!" Markita wagged her index finger in the air, her laughter dry and rapid, like the sound of moth wings flapping. "Didn't that *Psycho* guy have a dead mama, too?"

"Now you're being nasty. Fay told me that he cared for his mother's every need after she got the Alzheimer's. Cooked for her. Bathed her. Did everything and more—and for over ten years, to his own neglect."

"Nolan doesn't seem to think too much of him. Says Richard is flipped out on drugs or something. That he is out of touch with reality. That he talks a whole lot of nonsense and trash." Markita eyed another shrimp. "May I?" She waited for Doreen to nod before stabbing one. "How long has his mama been dead, anyway?"

"At least five years. She died before we moved here." Doreen stirred the stew. "Being that devoted to your mama seems more sweet and delicate than crazy to me."

"You mean 'delicate'?" Markita sashayed around the kitchen, flipping her wrists.

"Markita Calvo! We're all God's children! Since when have you been that way?"

"All I know is, grieving that long don't seem right. And I certainly wouldn't go trusting him around Curtis. That *Psycho* guy seemed pretty harmless, too, until he threw open the shower curtain."

Doreen smirked while ladling a few scoops of her stew into a china bowl. She covered it with plastic wrap and handed it to her friend. "You ever heard of something called a balsamic moon?" Her tone had shifted to one of seriousness.

"A balsamic—moon? Nope, never did." Markita flashed a precocious grin as she scooped up another shrimp.

"Sorry," Doreen said as she clamped a lid on top of the pot. "The rest is for Richard."

"Okay, okay. Go earn your saintly bonus points. Just be aware, will you?"

Be aware. Like the fortune-teller's warning. Doreen felt a strange unease as she watched Markita slip out the door, patting the bowl filled with stew as though it were a baby's bottom.

Richard sat in his disheveled living room playing Verdi's *Requiem* louder than usual, which was always fairly loud. Volume fueled the music's magic, providing the intensity to free him from his earthly confines. To aid in this escape, he often wore a pair of cardboard ear extenders he'd concocted by curving pliable panels of a Saltine box and attaching them to one of his mother's old headbands. They served as funnels, capturing the sound, and directing it inward. He closed his eyes and followed the music, enthralled, letting the repetitions of the Kyrie lift him out of his weary body. "Kyrie Eleison. Christe Eleison." *Lord have mercy on us. Christ have mercy on us.* He'd nearly fallen into a trance when a knock at his front door interrupted and startled him. He would not have responded had he not recognized Doreen's voice calling his name. Only then did he part the yellowing curtains and peek outside to double-check. His neighbor stood on his stoop holding a brown paper grocery bag.

Richard slowly cracked open his front door, allowing stale air to pour out along with the deafeningly loud music, and causing Doreen's smile to evaporate. When she saw Richard's cardboard ears, however, her face crinkled, trying unsuccessfully to suppress a giggle.

Unaware of the source of Doreen's amusement, but conscious of his bed hair and beard stubble, Richard wanted to shrink. Once upon a time he had attended to his physical appearance, in fact was quite fastidious, but no longer. He ran fingers over his unshaven chin and unruly eyebrows.

Seeing his discomfort, Doreen glanced away as he fumbled and clutched his robe. "Not feeling well, sugar?" she asked sympathetically.

He lowered his head and looked at his feet, flummoxed. "Never do anymore."

Doreen touched his arm and smiled. "Brought something that should fix you up." She held the brown bag out to give to him. "Creole shrimp stew. My mama's recipe. Just made it this morning."

Richard froze in place. "For me?"

"What's the matter? Don't you like shrimp stew?"

Her unexpected kindness confused him. He held his bathrobe closed as he bowed modestly. "Thank you," was the best response he could manage, then added, "I can't invite you in." He joined Doreen on the landing and pulled the door partially shut behind him. "The house is a mess. Mother was sick for a long time. Her bed is still in the middle of the living room floor. I can't move it. It's too heavy and I have a bad back."

"Maybe I could help you sometime."

Richard nodded, unable to think of a clever way to decline the offer. Even if he had wanted to move it, which he didn't because it served as a shrine, Richard would never have allowed anyone inside his sanctuary.

Doreen rocked, shifting from one foot to the other. Richard figured she was trying to get a glimpse inside, so he rocked along with her, mirroring her movements to block her view. "Hope you didn't go to too much trouble," he said, holding up the bag.

"Me? No. I love to cook. Plan on doing more today. It's a good distraction. Heck, if you can think of anything else you want?" She paused. "Just out of curiosity, what is your favorite food?"

A smile appeared on Richard's lips as he turned his eyes skyward. "Frog legs, I guess."

Doreen reeled. "You eat frogs!" She shook her head, then contorted her face and stuck out her tongue. "I don't even want to think about eating frogs!" She took a careful step back and shook her hands in the air. "Listen, sugar, I gotta run. Lots to do in case that hurricane comes our way." She turned and headed toward her house. "Don't worry about returning the container," she called back when she reached her walkway. "I'll come pick it up some other time."

Richard watched her leave. Once certain she'd gone into her home, he returned inside his, shut the door, and threw the bolt. *Eating frogs.* He laughed more heartily than he had in years. He figured telling her that would send her packing. Nice as Doreen had been to make him food, Richard was wary and didn't much appreciate having anyone drop over unannounced. He carried the stew into his kitchen, got a teaspoon from the drawer, and took a cautious bite. He smiled with delight and took several more spoonfuls before sliding it into the refrigerator uncovered, figuring he'd have the rest that evening. Though delicious, and glad to have it, he wondered why, after years of rarely exchanging more than a few words, had he become the recipient of such unprecedented largesse?

DAY THREE
Sunday, August 28

A long and restless night. Richard returned to bed that morning, craving more rest. He had almost tumbled over the edge of consciousness when persistent banging pulled him back from much-needed sleep. He flinched. Hugged his pillow when he recognized Nolan Lagusi bellowing through his front door. That voice still turned his stomach and made his throat tighten. Richard forced himself out of bed and into the alcove between his bedroom and bathroom, a place where he couldn't be seen through any window. He leaned against the cool plaster wall and tried to shake off his fatigue. He rubbed his scratchy eyes and heavy lids and resisted the desire to smoke.

"Richard, you in there?" Nolan Lagusi pressed his weatherworn face against the small round window in the front door. "Fay and me, we're going to Baton Rouge. We want you to come with us." His neighbor's bony fist pounded against the door. "It'd be like old times having you along." He rattled the knob. "Come on, son, answer your goddamn door."

Go to hell! Richard's heartbeat echoed in his ears. He curled his toes under, digging them into the carpet as if standing on sand at the beach as a big wave approached. He held on tight. After a few minutes of cursing and name-calling, Nolan finally left. A short time later the phone rang. Richard let it ring. He wasn't about to get into a conversation. It wasn't until he heard the Lagusi's old Pontiac sputter down the street that he finally took a deep breath.

After spending all morning searching for an open store that had more candles and bottles of water to sell, Doreen was frustrated, irritable, and beat. She spread out the supplies she'd purchased on her kitchen counter, inspected them, and then poured the remainder of this morning's sweetened coffee over ice. She sipped it and plopped down in front of the television. The talk on every station was about the hurri-cane—where and when it might hit as it approached landfall. As anxious as this made her, Doreen had to admit that she did like the storm's name. Katrina sounded like a perky young skater or the tinkle of ice cubes in a tall cool drink, though the National Weather Service warned that the storm was now a Category Five—highest on the scale and most dangerous. Katrina had grown into a storm of extraordinary scope and strength.

Until yesterday morning, the storm had been projected to come ashore near Mobile, Alabama, but the track had shifted westward, placing New Orleans squarely in her path. Local reporters had spread throughout the low-lying city, interview-ing nervous residents and visitors. Many people had already evacuated but plenty of others had no way out. Flights were booked solid, leaving some tourists with no choice but to stay. Lots of locals didn't own cars or have the financial abil-ity to go elsewhere. "Leave how? Go where?" they asked. Others were remaining to protect property, or to care for sick or elderly relatives who could not be moved. Medical person-nel, government employees, and some who worked in service industries were staying behind because of job responsibili-ties. More than a few had concerns about leaving beloved pets. One couple noted the balmy, tranquil weather and boasted of planning a hurricane party with friends.

Doreen could not shake Mercy's ominous prediction— *the bad fortune around you will not go away but will grow.* Though she doubted the woman's clairvoyance, especially considering her bizarre balsamic moon remark, her words continued to haunt. *A bunch of mumbo jumbo,* she kept telling herself. *All those fortune-tellers downtown are phonies.* A balsamic moon sounded like some silly Italian curse or Cajun superstition. *Everything will be fine. The storm has already turned a couple of times. No doubt it'll turn again.* Nevertheless, the radar images on the Weather Channel and satellite photos from space had her mesmerized. She continually flipped between television stations, catching reports about the storm's progress and preparations being taken by people throughout the Gulf Coast. She watched so intently that when the phone rang, she jumped and spilled her coffee on the counter. "Hello?" she said breathlessly, as she tore off a paper towel to mop the brown puddle.

"You listening to the news, baby doll?" her father asked. "They're saying it could be bad, that we could get hit hard this time."

"They're paid to make it sound like that, Daddy."

"Your mama was sick most of the night. Don't think she could handle the drive up to your Aunt Anita's. Me and your sisters are taking her to the Superdome this afternoon instead. City's turning it into a public shelter. We want you to come meet us there."

Doreen pictured a stadium teeming with all sorts of unsavory people. "Know what, Daddy? Think I'll stay put. Sleep in my own bed. I've got plenty of food and water. I don't want to leave my house. What if Curtis calls?"

"Thought you said he was staying upstate."

"I heard they're not going to allow people to bring pets. We have this dog now. I've made a safe place for us in the bathroom. Even filled up the tub, just in case we need extra water."

"But what if you needed help or, God forbid, got hurt?"

"The guy next door is sticking around. Others will, too. Don't worry. I'll be fine."

Doreen heard her mother's voice in the background. "Tell her she *has* to come with us."

"Why don't y'all come over here. My house is lots newer than yours, and it's in Gentilly. This is higher ground. I got plenty of food and water. Even got extra candles. Come here."

"The Superdome was made to stand up to hurricanes," her father countered. "We've already packed pillows, blankets, and Mama's medicines. Come meet us there. It's only for one night."

"No, Daddy. Thanks, but I'm staying put."

"For the life of me, I don't know where you got such a hard head!"

Doreen laughed. "Don't you?" Her dad chuckled, too.

After hanging up, she channeled her nervous energy into cleaning the house. While sweeping her floors, she distracted herself by sending good wishes to her ailing mother, and recalling her mother's lady friends who'd attended church with their family when she was a girl. Both she and her mother cherished New Orleans' strong black communities; they provided such great support, acceptance, and connection. She smiled as she pictured the fantasia of hats the ladies wore, and how the women would nod to one another in tribute and friendly competition. Their hats had been works of art. Helene Mitchell, one of her mother's closest friends and chief rivals, had been famous for her Easter bonnets. Even now the thought of one of her hats had Doreen laughing out loud. It was completely covered in white feathers. When she wore it, she looked like a chicken had nested on top of her head.

The next time the phone rang Doreen grew prickly. Did her father think he could keep calling and get her to change her mind? "Okay, Daddy, now what?" she asked, employing a wisecracking tone.

"Looks like Katrina's going to slam right into us." It was Markita on the line, sounding uncharacteristically restrained and serious. "Pack a bag. We're coming to get you."

"How are you going to leave? All the gas stations are closed. And they're saying traffic's so heavy it takes more than eight hours just to get to Baton Rouge. Think it's safer staying put. Besides, I don't have enough money to do this again." She waited. There was no response. Doreen wondered if the phone might have gone dead. "You there, Kita?" She heard Markita begin to weep. "Hey, no, don't do that. Talk to me."

"Leave with us, Dory. Please," Markita pleaded. "Sam got us a full tank of gas. I got a horrible feeling about you staying here. Like it's a nightmare starting to come true. Just leave with us and don't worry about the money. We'll figure that out."

"Hush now. I can't go running off. Mama and Daddy are heading downtown to the Superdome. What if they need me? And there's Buddy." Doreen looked down at the light-colored dog who sat beside her. "You and Sam go on ahead. I'll be fine. I got plenty of stuff here—canned red beans, power bars, crackers, lots of candles. If things get too bad, I'll tuck myself into the bathroom and pull towels over me."

By the end of the call both women had fallen apart. Doreen could barely breathe between sobs. She abandoned her cleaning frenzy and headed to her bedroom, searching the top drawer of her dresser for a photograph. She sat on her bed, clicked on the bedside light, and gazed at a picture of two girls standing side by side at age eight. Although the two were wearing matching outfits sewn by Markita's mother, they couldn't have appeared more different. Markita—darker and taller, with knobby knees and a big toothy grin—dwarfed plump little Doreen. Markita's deep brown eyes receded, while Doreen's incongruent green eyes stared out from the photo. Markita looked angelic, shy, and sweet, like she'd never done anything wrong in her life. Doreen's demeanor was much the opposite—hands cinching her waist and a mocking, mischievous expression on her face.

Doreen returned to the kitchen, questioning the wisdom of staying, as well as her resolve. Then she took note of the kitchen wallpaper that she'd put up herself. Bright red poppies. Bold. Cheerful. *Damnit,* she told herself, *this was her home.* It had taken her seven long years of sharing a room with her sisters while she lived with her parents. Seven years ignoring pretty dresses in store windows. Seven years of taking bagged lunches to work, and squirreling away every extra nickel. But she'd done it; saved enough money for a down payment. Her pregnancy might have been unplanned, but her life certainly wasn't. Doreen had a well-drawn road map and its first stop had been owning a home of her own.

When she recounted the obligations she felt to her house, to her family, and to the sweet snoring dog sleeping soundly at her feet, leaving her Gentilly neighborhood seemed impractical and irresponsible. She had made her decision. Storm warnings be damned. She was staying put.

Richard flipped through his extensive collection and selected the vinyl recording he had been thinking about all morning. He lovingly removed the record from its well-preserved jacket and protective plastic sleeve, and placed it on his turntable. He sat and removed his thick eyeglasses, awaiting the sound of an orchestra to surge forward; once it had, he held his breath in anticipation as a woman's anguished cry pierced the air. Maria Callas. He adored the way that she left notes dangling and conveyed emotion with the slightest shift of vibrato. His head swayed, feeling the kinship of their shared, real-life miseries. Richard considered Callas a soulmate. She had died alone and wanting, of a broken heart.

He knew all too well what it meant to have life whittled down, to be without; understood the toll it took on one's spirit and soul. Years of devoting himself to his mother's care had resulted in a life of isolation, losing touch with old friends and fearful that he'd grown too old and withdrawn to make new ones. His world had grown small. It had contracted on itself. The most he hoped for now was to read, listen to music, and live his remaining years in peace. He had settled for watching the world turn through his living-room window, and looking after the neighborhood children at play while keeping a vigilant eye on the Lagusi's garage directly across the street.

Richard had nearly lost himself to the music when he heard Doreen's voice calling to him once again from outside his front door. Though tempted to ignore her, the urgency she conveyed propelled him from his chair. He needed a moment to crank his body into an upright position. Going from a sitting position to a standing one hurt. Every day his creaky spine became less flexible and standing upright more problematic.

Richard opened the door part way, bracing it from behind with his arm and foot. Doreen's light-brown complexion had flushed crimson red. Beads of perspiration dotted her forehead and upper lip like tiny, raised freckles. She stepped forward and handed him his newspaper, bouncing up and down on the balls of her feet as though she were about to explode. "So, you don't just deliver food, but newspapers, too?" He consciously employed a smile while not easing his hold on the door.

"You heard, didn't you?" she blurted. "What are you going to do now?"

"Heard what?" he asked, shaking his head.

"Mayor just made the evacuation mandatory."

Richard glanced at the headline of *The Times-Picayune.* "Katrina Takes Aim." An aerial color photo placed above the banner showed an enormous white mass sitting over the bright blue waters in the Gulf. A red arrow indicated the storm's expected path, which took it directly over the city of New Orleans.

"The son-of-a-bitch can't do that!" Richard threw open his door and joined Doreen outside.

"Just did, on television, with Governor Blanco standing right beside him. I saw it."

"I never heard of such foolishness. What are they going to do, send out police? Shoot us for staying in our own homes?"

"You're talking New Orleans cops!" Her eyes filled with tears. "They just might."

"Yeah, well, I've got a rifle stashed in the attic, and I'd use it if they tried a stunt like that!"

Doreen's lower jaw dropped. Her green eyes spilled tears as they widened. Richard immediately regretted mentioning the rifle; he'd meant to reassure her, not scare her. "Hey," he said, holding up his hands as though surrendering, with both palms in full sight. "Not to worry. I won't be climbing any bell towers or anything."

Doreen backed down his steps, her mouth agape. "Of course, all right. Everything's good. I'd better get back to my house. Lots of stuff to do." She streaked the tears on her face by wiping them with her palms. "You take care. I'll catch up with you later, okay?"

Richard stood in place and watched Doreen leave before returning inside his house and sitting in his high-backed chair. He removed his thick eyeglasses and held a large magnifying glass over the newspaper. *An extreme storm,* he read.

Monday landfall likely as a strong Category 4. The lead article was made more emphatic by its subtitle—*Katrina bulks up to become a perfect storm.* His stomach soured as he thought about how unprepared both he and his city were for what might be coming.

Once he'd moved past the screaming headlines, Richard flipped through several pages to peruse the obituary column, as was his custom. Years ago, he'd discovered that reading of others' losses made him feel a little less lonely. However, his cursory scan this time took an unexpected turn when he tripped over a familiar name—someone he hadn't seen in almost twenty years. René Kilpatrick had died several days earlier. The cause of death, a lung infection; his age, fifty-six.

Richard set the newspaper down on the tabletop and smoothed its creases, glancing at the ceiling. His lower lip quivered. Tears fell. Reading the notice of René's death tapped into woefully sad memories. He closed his eyes and recalled René's impishly endearing personality, ruddy complexion, stick-out ears, self-effacing humor, and goofy little laugh. Though he hadn't thought of René in a long time, reading of his death made him feel that much more alone. Yet another loss. Too much to take.

Doreen continually checked the clock. Its hands had hardly moved. *Amazing how slow time goes by when you're anticipating something bad. Even more slowly than when waiting for something good.* She snickered at the irony. The air had grown still and thick; the humidity supersaturating, even more than usual. The world outside had grown eerily quiet. Most of her neighbors had left town. She could hear none of the traffic noises usually coming from Elysian Fields Avenue, the four-lane thoroughfare two blocks away. The birds, which most always sang or squawked, had gone silent. That added another dimension to her nervousness. She distracted herself by playing solitaire for a while but couldn't stay focused. She went into the kitchen, ate a chocolate bar, and rearranged the canned goods in her pantry, turning labels forward. After that she vacuumed the carpets. As a light rain started falling, she spread out papers on the kitchen table and worked on her lesson plans for the first week of school. But Katrina was never far from her thoughts. The buildup to this storm's arrival had been like a drum roll that went on and on, growing ever louder. Katrina had started to show herself, at least the hem of her skirt had, and more of her was on the way. Doreen avoided looking out the windows as if ignoring the weather might make the storm go away. Mercy's prediction of tragedy and hard times loomed larger now that all she could do was wait, on her own, and without Curtis. Evening approached; the outside was growing dark. The outermost bands of the hurricane had begun to make their presence felt in the city. And, if that wasn't frightening enough, she'd learned from her odd, perhaps mentally unbalanced neighbor, that he kept a rifle in his attic.

She had assembled more than adequate supplies of water and non-perishable foods. Even if it took a week for things to get back to normal, such basics should not be a problem. Like money in the bank. She looked at her stash frequently, drawing comfort from knowing it was there. But she also knew that plenty of disastrous things could happen. She could lose her windows or her roof, or the house itself might collapse on top of her. She wondered if the sadness Mercy spoke of in her tarot reading—due to the passing of an Empress, "someone held most dear"—was a prediction that she would die in the storm, that Curtis would be left without a mother. Tears rolled down her cheeks.

Doreen turned on the television. Newscasters continued to shout warnings and suggest precautions for viewers who remained in the city. Weathermen stood outside, exposed to the elements, where they would be blasted by the elements for added drama. Wind gusts had started whipping up the rain. Agitated by what she saw, Doreen shut off the TV again and focused her attention on Buddy, grateful for his company. *When Curtis sees you, he's going to be the happiest kid on the planet!*

She played with Buddy for quite a while, scratching his ears and rubbing his stomach, as the light drumming of rain grew harder and louder, and the time between squalls shorter. Occasionally, the wind slammed against the house with such force that it rattled windows and doors. Doreen left the dog to confirm that every window in the house was securely shut. Buddy followed right behind her. Whenever the wind shook the trees, or she heard the sharp drumming of a particularly insistent downpour, she whispered the word, "no!" as if she could tell the storm to go away. *Storms almost always turn.* She understood that this one might not.

It had grown late. Though tired, the adrenalin surging through her body would not allow her to stay in one place, much less sleep. She saw no reason to try. She paced with Buddy in tow, returning to each window, checking that the blinds and curtains were closed. Should glass shatter, closed curtains might stop shards from flying into the house. She led

Buddy into her entry hall and paused in front of a wall filled with family photos. She made him sit and then pointed to pictures of Curtis. "That's your boy," she told the dog. "You two are going to be great friends. He needs a friend like you." Curtis had few friends and was often teased at school. It concerned her. She thought of how he had whined about being sent to a sports camp. He didn't want to go. He was hardly athletic; he preferred reading and singing in the choir. She worried about her boy being soft. It was a tough world out there and Curtis was definitely a mama's boy. Her fault? Perhaps. She told herself that she'd kept him close for his safety and well-being, but wondered if it hadn't also been to keep her own loneliness at bay.

She raised her hand and touched an old daguerreotype that hung high on the wall. "Now that you're part of the family, I'll give you a little history lesson." She smiled when Buddy cocked his head as though truly trying to take this in. "That's the man who started it all." She pointed to the picture of an elderly white-haired fellow sitting on a garden bench with three young boys beside him. "Henri Reynard, my great grandfather." She patted Buddy's smooth, broad head. "I know. He almost looks white. That's because he was—half. That's how I got these eyes." Buddy looked at her, as though listening intently. "He arrived here from Martinique, a free person of color. Settled in the Faubourg Marigny. Created his very own plaster works business. Built himself a fine old house. The house is still there, but it doesn't belong to our family anymore." She shook her head. "Monsieur Reynard did well. He had his own cook, and everything. Those little boys with him were his grandsons. The one with the glasses, Albert, was my granddaddy. He went to school up north and returned home a licensed doctor."

She turned and peeked through the small window in her front door. Conditions outside were deteriorating. Wind shook the window sashes and rattled the doors with greater insistence. Occasionally, she heard a low moan that sounded much like a train whistle. She double-checked the bolt on her front door, making certain that it was latched and secure. For good measure, she pushed the coffee table from her living room against the door and shoved a chair up behind that. Was it her imagination, or did the door seem to bend slightly as it resisted the wind? Frightening. Doreen shut her eyes, said a quick prayer, and then returned her focus to her family's pictures. She had told Buddy to stay, and he had. "Good boy." She stroked his head. "These here are Daddy's people." She pointed. "Several worked as house servants." She straightened the framed photo of a stiff middle-aged couple dressed in their modest Sunday best and looking very uncomfortable. She chuckled. "These two characters were my daddy's grandparents."

As she lowered her hand, a thunderous noise reverberated through the house. She crouched reflexively, cursing. Certain that something large had fallen through her kitchen ceiling, she braced herself for more, while screaming, "No!" as though delivering a command. When nothing else happened, she cautiously stood and moved in the direction of the noise, pulling a hesitant Buddy by the collar toward the kitchen. She entered, expecting to see all kinds of damage, but found none. Then another, even louder crash came from above. She screamed. Buddy shook and whimpered with fear. Doreen didn't wait to see what might have happened. She again grabbed hold of Buddy by the collar, this time dragging him toward the bathroom. Confused and scared, Buddy resisted. His legs stiffened, but Doreen would not yield. She brought the dog inside the bathroom and slammed the door shut behind them. The frequency and volume of noises outside had suddenly increased; things had started crashing against the house, knocking on it from every direction. She pulled the plug on the bathtub to drain the water, believing a secure hiding place far more important than having an extra stash of water. As the tub emptied, she gathered towels and clothes she'd taken from cabinets and hampers, and piled them on the floor. She lifted the hefty dog inside the bathtub, climbed in with him, and began piling layers of the towels and clothes over them both. Buddy tried to wiggle out of her grasp as she pressed their bodies against the hard wet enamel of the cast-iron basin, but the dog's struggles to free himself from confinement only made her clutch him more firmly. Eventually, he relented with a sigh.

Towels and blankets did little to buffer the increasing roar surrounding them. The whistles and howls of the wind had grown far louder. The storm wanted in; it tried to force its way through every closed window and doorjamb, as well as the floorboards. *Dear Lord,* she prayed, *please protect me. Let me see my boy again. I miss him so. Allow me to help him grow up to be a good and righteous man. Let me know my grandchildren. Let them be people of conscience and character.* Within minutes, the clatter outside increased far further, sounding like metal trashcans falling on top of her house. *I don't understand how this can be happening so fast!* She squeezed her eyes shut and continued to pray.

DAY FOUR
Monday, August 29

Yesterday afternoon, Richard had watched clouds thicken until they resembled rumpled wool blankets. Now, as midnight passed, he thought of them more as shrouds. The barometric pressure had steadily dropped, causing his sinuses and the spaces behind his eyes to swell and grow puffy. He wondered how the rhythmic pinging of raindrops hitting against the windowpanes might sound driven with full hurricane force.

All summer long, he'd eagerly awaited the arrival of a storm, hoping for fantastic displays of lightning. Prayed for it. And now a storm was here. He met it with great anticipation. Nothing got his blood flowing faster. But as this storm continued to intensify and become more threatening, he grew wary and began to have doubts. Late afternoon thunderstorms in New Orleans interrupted the city's intense heat; they were predictable, legendary, and even literary. Tennessee Williams had written one into his play, *A Streetcar Named Desire*. But this summer, the weather hadn't followed its usual pattern; it unfolded strangely. The frequent thunderstorms, whose rain refreshed and whose lightning provided moments of excitement in Richard's otherwise dull life, hadn't come. The heat had never broken, and the sub-tropical landscape had grown increasingly distressed.

Wearing his cardboard ear extenders to magnify the music and compete with the noises raging outside, Richard gingerly slipped a record onto his turntable. An operatic voice sang, "*Mi chiamo Fedeltà. Un soffio è la mia voce che al nuovo dì morrà ...*" Reading the translation in the libretto from *Adriana Lecouvreur*, Richard sighed with sympathetic resignation, embracing the drama of it, believing that he, too, could have been called Faithfulness, and that his voice might also die on the morrow.

To a casual listener, the beauty of Cilèa's aria might have masked its bitter poignancy, but Richard never listened to music casually. Music delivered messages—some reflective, others predictive—and at this moment it shifted his perspective from eager anticipation to a dark revelation of massive destruction, soon to come. Katrina's vehemence would overwhelm his city, and no force of will or denial could prevent it. *If I die in the storm, would anyone know? Would anyone care? Would anyone even check to see if I had?* At that moment, feelings of isolation beyond anything he'd previously experienced gripped him. He sat in the living room on the frame of his mother's metal hospital bed, knowing his life had been emptied out. He had no one to rely upon or complain to; no one to phone—not family or friends.

The mechanical sling he used to transfer his mother from bed to chair and back again dangled its seat from a shiny chrome chain. The chain swayed slightly, looking much like a hangman's rope. He envisioned his body suspended from it, eyes bulging. He shook his head to erase that haunting image while rolling onto his side and drawing his knees against his chest. He lay on the bed, immobilized, until he decided he needed to change the music. He got up and, with practiced precision, set the stylus on a recording of *Tosca*, initiating the third act so he could listen to Cavaradossi sing to his beloved from a prison cell. Richard teared up, waiting for him to recite the last line of the letter he'd written to her, *E non ho amato mai tanto la vita*— "And never have I loved life so much"— a sentiment that he was astonished to share at this moment.

Antsy and increasingly anxious, Richard walked to the hall closet and retrieved an overcoat that had belonged to his father. He wrapped the coat around his arm, trying to establish a physical connection to him. That gave him the idea that he might use his parents' possessions to conduct a séance, while simultaneously satisfying his desire for distraction at such an unnerving time. Though he had no expectation that a séance would work, he did hope it might make his parents feel closer, and less like memories. As the clanging and banging outside grew louder, he moved through the house, investigating drawers and closets, reading old notes in his parents' handwriting that were scribbled on scraps of paper, and checking in forgotten areas of bookshelves for odds and ends in order to accumulate poignant memorabilia with purposeful and otherworldly intent. He scoured the bathroom, taking his father's safety razor, which he believed might still have bits of DNA remaining on it, as well as a horse syringe Richard had used to feed his mother—having filled it with pureed foods and squirting it into her mouth when she could no longer chew solids. He placed these items among other things gathered on top of the kitchen table.

Ignoring the groaning of wind and thumping of rain, he reached into a cupboard above the kitchen sink, his fingers seeking a cream-colored porcelain mug that years ago had been turned upside down and pushed to the very back of the highest shelf. The mug, which touted the city of New Orleans as host of the 1984 World's Fair, had been his mother's favorite. "The City Care Forgot," it boasted. Richard crushed out a cigarette as he thought of the first time he had seen his mother become catatonic and unresponsive. The two had been sitting together at the breakfast table. She grew motionless, almost like a statue, with this very mug poised at her lips. A detached vacant look had eclipsed her usual morning behaviors and comical grumbles, a look that would eventually be familiar, originating somewhere behind her eyes. He made certain that neither of them drank from that accursed mug ever again.

Rain now beat on the roof and sides of the house with such force that it sometimes drowned out the blare of his music. Richard scooped up all these belongings and carried them into the living room, where he set them on the carpet. The wind, howling as fiercely as a chorus of banshees, reinforced his sense of urgency, propelling him to stand and find more. A short while later, he knelt surrounded by mounds of shoes, scarves, lipstick tubes, and jewelry; handkerchiefs, tie tacks, belts, penknives, and nail clippers. He inspected each with great reverence, as though every one of them was an object from a museum's precious collection. Grateful to still have the benefits of electricity and lights, he took his time, first sorting these keepsakes by the parent they'd belonged to, then by their purpose, and after that by his own personal attachment to each, placing aside those that seemed less significant, until he had whittled the total number of objects to eleven.

He sought a twelfth—twelve being the number of apostles, months in a year, hours on the clock, and signs of the zodiac. He selected a black bobby pin that had belonged to the nurse who had tended to his mother when she died in the hospital. "Judas," he snarled under his breath as he twirled the bobby pin tightly between his fingers.

After arranging the twelve objects in a circle, he lowered himself into the center and began shifting them around, noting whenever the rain eased or increased, testing to see if the arrangements had any effect, and about the possibility of creating good and bad omens. He used brief moments of relative calm to write notes on handmade tags, attaching them to the objects they described, believing that they would let others know their significance and understand. His first tag read, "The last shoe mother wore before becoming bedridden." He wheezed slightly, his breathing constricted by his tight chest and cigarette clogged lungs, as his fingers traced the impressions of her toes and heel inside the soft blue leather moccasin—tangible evidence of the person lost to him.

As Katrina's fury intensified to a full-throated rage, all chaos and jumble, Richard turned off every light and pushed the living-room curtains open all the way. He sat as though before a movie screen, hoping to convert the experience to one of entertainment, surrounded as he was by his circle of protective trinkets, and anticipating dramatic bolts of lightning. But he only saw rain illuminated by streetlight. At least the rain didn't disappoint. It fell hard and sideways, pushed by the wind. It pelted against the window. He measured the increasing strength of the wind gusts by watching the trees in front of his house sway, bend, and shake.

Smoking helped Richard pass the time. He lit each cigarette with the stub of the last, frequently exhaling a series of smoke rings and poking at them as they drifted away. In the course of several hours, he played the complete recording of *Les Troyens*, repeating the aria, "Adieu Fière Cité," three times. Every so often he'd stick his head out the back door and call for Blanche, willing to give the cat refuge inside. The rain stung like buckshot and obscured the view through his thick eyeglasses. His thin hair thrashed and flogged his forehead. Eventually, he quit. Continuing to call for her was futile; she had probably sought protection, perhaps under the house. Nevertheless, he knew how guilty he'd feel if anything happened to her.

Believing it possible that his choice of music might influence atmospheric events, he shifted from opera to symphonic compositions by Brahms and Beethoven, selecting works that rivaled the turbulence of the weather as the wind sprayed rain into misty veils and spirals that glowed under the streetlights, shimmering gauze woven with threads of nickel—silvery dark. Despite wearing his cardboard ears to amplify the music's impact and distract from the whooshing of the wind, the random booms and crashes outside added a frightful barrage of percussive noises that reminded him of a child with a new set of drums, banging away without the slightest concern for rhythm. At least the electricity had not gone out. He took comfort and resolve in that. Changing musical direction once again, he decided the best soundtrack to accompany the events outside might be playing Wagner, full blast, letting his opera build and his maiden warriors sing their stirring battle cry. "Hojotoho!" The mythic Valkyries would match the storm's wrath; they could defy winds that rattled doors and window casings like thieves testing points of entry. "Ho-jotoho!" But when something big smashed against his living-room window, cracking the glass with a sound as shockingly earsplitting as a gunshot, Richard leaped from his seat, pulled the curtains closed, and laid down on the floor, placing his hands behind his head like a prisoner of war.

Simultaneously with Wagner's musical crescendo, the walls of his house began to heave. From his prone position on the carpet, he stared in fearful amazement as the large oval mirror hanging above the sofa swayed and scraped against the plaster wall. Then, the whole house started trembling as though caught in an earthquake. Terror made moving imper-ative but provided no direction. *Where do I go? What do I do?* He stood and spun in place, then grabbed hold of his mother's mattress and dragged it into his bedroom, ignoring the protests registering in his recalcitrant back. He threw open the door to his closet, shoved clothes aside, and pulled the mattress in with him to provide a buffer by wedging himself behind it. *Enough! Make it stop! Please, Mother, make it stop!*

Within minutes inside the airless closet, his skin grew clammy. Sweat poured from his head and brow. A metallic taste in his mouth preceded a ball of heat that originated in his stomach and rose to the top of his head. An upheaval of nausea followed. Distraught, he kicked open the closet door and lunged forward in a dash for the bathroom, tripping over the mattress as his body convulsed. He vomited on the carpet and down the front of his tee-shirt. Scrambling onto his feet, he staggered to the bathroom, eager to remove the stench, and to throw water on his face, but instead of running water he heard only gurgling sounds and clanking like a metal pipe struck several times with a heavy wrench. He was about to try turning on the tub faucets when the beams above his head began screeching and creaking. He knew what that meant; the music had warned him. His heart pounded so hard he wondered if he might be having a heart attack. A low groan escaped his lips as he raced back into his bedroom, imploring his parents for protection. While diving inside the closet again, and squeezing his body behind the plastic-coated mattress, he heard a loud pop followed by a thud. The world went black. The electricity had finally cut out.

The range of threatening noises sounded more menacing cloaked in total darkness. He jammed fingers in his ears, longing for deafness to accompany his blindness. He knelt and prayed that, if this was to be his end, it would come quickly and without pain—that a bolt of lightning would strike him and take him away, reunite him with his parents. He counted aloud. "One, two, three, four, five, six, seven, eight, nine, ten. One, two, three, four…" Over and over; anything to escape the din outside the house and inside his head. His eyes shut so tightly that he saw a kaleidoscope of geometric patterns. Without music to bolster him, he feared collapse. Then it came to him. He hadn't lost the music entirely. He could still sing. But the one song that kept coming to mind offered no comfort. "You Can't Always Get What You Want," by the Rolling Stones.

He hugged his mother's mattress as hope drained from his heart. His parents were gone. René was gone. He could not be more utterly alone—alone wearing a puke-stained tee-shirt and cowering in a storm on the floor of a closet.

Curled inside the bathtub underneath layers of towels, clothes, and blankets, Doreen wept in the darkness, overwhelmed by screaming noises assaulting her from outside, and thinking of how she preferred Richard's operas to Katrina's shrieks. She held on to Buddy, who remained compliant. She feared that the walls of her house would cave in on them, and for more than an hour they threatened to do just that—creaking, cracking, and groaning as Katrina tried to pry loose every nail and screw in the place.

She thought of Mercy, the tarot card reader—old, blind, and frail. Had she and others like her found safe harbor? Had they been provided transportation elsewhere before the storm arrived? As the cacophony closed in, fear and avoidance drove her deeper into reflection. She remembered how, with her father's encouragement during her college years, she'd earned honors along with her degree. And how her mother's prediction that she would never marry had crushed her. Doreen spent years trying to prove her father right and her mother wrong, becoming self-reliant—a teacher repeatedly rewarded for professional excellence—and of how she'd wasted six precious years in union with the man who would eventually abandon her—Curtis's biological father—a man without substance, whose charm and good looks had been his only assets.

As the hurricane's roar quieted, Buddy grew increasingly agitated, squirming and whimpering. He wanted out. Doreen peeled back the layers covering them and gazed into the oyster-gray light of morning. She listened, trying to interpret the quiet, cautiously wondering if the worst of the storm had passed. Only when convinced they could leave the safety of the tub did she release Buddy. He leaped from her grasp onto the bathroom floor, shaking his body from head to tail several times. She stood, walked to the bathroom window, and peered outside. Relief had her weeping with gratitude. The winds and rain had most definitely decreased. Loose debris, sections of gutter, and fallen tree limbs littered lawns and walkways. Puddles of standing water filled potholes on both sides of the road. Cars were strewn with leaves and downed branches. Across the street, the Lagusi's rickety old garage had toppled. But the scene was not nearly as apocalyptic as she'd feared. The world outside the walls of her home may have been a disheveled mess but most of it remained essentially intact.

She went to check on the other rooms of her house with Buddy following behind. Rain had leaked through the kitchen ceiling. Chalky-colored water pooled in the middle of the floor. She flipped on the light switch to get a better view, but there was no electricity. Then, without thinking, she tried the radio. It worked. She heard a weak, barely audible signal. *Batteries. Damn, I should have bought more of them. These must be ancient. I don't remember ever changing them.*

Doreen put her ear next to the radio and listened. An announcer talked about Katrina having turned, shifting east just before coming ashore; that the brunt of the storm had missed New Orleans and struck the border between Louisiana and Mississippi. New Orleans had been spared, but damage to Mississippi's shoreline communities was extensive. *Jesus! If that was a sideswipe, I can only imagine...*

Doreen ran to her telephone, desperate to contact someone at Curtis's camp, and to speak with her parents as well. Despite having a dial tone, her calls would not go through. By the time she gave up and returned to the radio, the batteries had quit. That came as no surprise. She moved to the threshold of her son's bedroom, aching to hold him. She stared at the two large pennants she'd chosen to decorate the wall above his bed—one of the New Orleans Saints and the other, the Atlanta Braves. On his desk, she found a dozen or more printed copies of Renaissance paintings and sculptures that Curtis had purchased with his allowance on a class field trip to the museum in City Park. Her son's interest in that kind of art mystified her, but she found reassurance browsing among the other more familiar items he kept on his dresser— model cars, a couple of rubber cockroaches, a Goo Goo Cluster candy wrapper, and specimens from his treasured rock and shell collection. Boy stuff. She missed him terribly. His absence filled the house.

She felt profound gratitude that her home had been spared. Losing power and having a leaky roof weren't so bad, all things considered. She was alive. Her world hadn't come to an end. The storm had passed. Curtis could make it home now without a problem. Life would return to normal in a day or two. Praise Jesus! New Orleans had dodged the bullet one more time. Though this was a city known to celebrate most everything with a cocktail, several of which had been created here, including Brandy Milk Punches and Sazeracs, Doreen had never been much of an alcohol drinker. This morning, however, after removing the coffee table and chair bracing her front door, and sending Buddy outside to relieve himself, she popped open a can of beer that Sam had left in her refrigerator many months earlier, raised it in the air, cheered the universe, and took a sip. She wasn't wild about the taste but had good reason to celebrate.

Richard lit a cigarette. Nicotine felt familiar and comforting in his lungs. He exhaled with lips pursed, sending out a thin gray line of smoke. Sitting in his chair, he tapped his fingertips to the calypso rhythms of the rain surging and retreating. Grayish-blue clouds covering the stormy sky ended abruptly to the south and west. The turbulence had ended, which was a relief, although he found it confounding and, in some measure, disappointing that a storm of such magnitude and force had eliminated the electricity without producing much lightning.

The first thing he noticed when surveying the scene outside was that the Lagusi's decrepit garage had come down—its boards, rafters, and roof shingles strewn across the lawns and driveways of neighboring homes. Richard rejoiced. Katrina had done everyone a favor. The Barnett's house down the block had lost a window—a Venetian blind blew in and out of its frame like a child's swing. Shutters on several of his neighbors' houses had been bent or hung askew. Awnings, roof tiles, and trash cans had been deposited everywhere. Detritus from plants and trees littered most of the neighborhood, but even with all that mess, things did not look catastrophic.

The damage inside his home was limited to the crack in his living-room window. The keepsakes he'd placed in a circle on the floor remained exactly as he'd left them. He smiled. Perhaps they had provided him some protection. He scooped them up and put them in an old shoebox, shoving the box under his bed, safely tucked away. With effort he pulled down the folding staircase attached to a ceiling panel in the hallway.

He climbed up and took stock of the attic. Except for a narrow shaft of light that shone through on its far side, which meant that the roof might have lost a tile or two, the attic appeared dry and undisturbed.

Confident that the interior of his house was secure, Richard continued his inspection, walking out of the house. Priority one, however, would be to check on Blanche.

Doreen, already outside, stood checking on the condition of her house with Buddy at her side. Richard saluted her from across their litter-strewn common strip of lawn. Doreen reacted by sprinting toward him, her arms outstretched and hands leading the way, the rain-soaked ground splashing under her sneakers. To his alarm, she wrapped her arms around him and gave him a bear hug. Standing on tiptoe, she kissed his cheek exuberantly.

Richard froze, unaccustomed to another person's touch. He had no idea what to say or do.

Doreen released him, tucking her blouse into her shorts. "Sorry. But I'm just so damn relieved." She blinked away tears and attempted a grin as she stepped back from him.

Richard forced himself to respond, though speaking felt unnatural, like a skill that had escaped him. "Yes," he answered, slightly above a whisper.

Doreen's voice cracked. "Jesus H. Christ! I've never prayed so hard in my life." She took another step back and looked around. "Can you believe it? The storm turned at the last minute. I knew it would. And are we lucky!" She patted the dog's head. His tail wagged. He looked as pleased as she was. "I heard that the towns along the Mississippi coast have been wiped off the map."

"Wait. You have power?" Richard asked.

She shook her head. "No, old batteries in a radio. They didn't last long."

"How about your phone?"

"Tried it first thing. Wanted to call my parents but couldn't get through." She gazed at Richard. "Forgive me for saying this, but you look even more tired than I feel. Bet I'm not the only one who hasn't slept much the last few nights." She yawned. "Well, I'd better get back to checking things out so that I can lay down. I'm beat." She waved goodbye as she led the dog across their wet common lawn to her front steps.

Richard continued walking along the side of his house, pausing to examine a section of siding that had peeled away from a corner. He wiggled its ragged edge back and forth. An aluminum awning that had shaded a window in the back of his house had been ripped from its supports; it rested against the chain-link fence in the backyard, upside down, filled with rainwater like a basin.

Richard called for Blanche. Getting no response, he knelt to search for her under the house, soaking both knees of his well-worn jeans as he crawled on all fours into the dark space. When something white streaked across the exposed foundation, he wasn't certain it was Blanche until he caught sight of the cat's reflective yellow eyes glinting at him. "There you are sweetie pie. Hi. I was worried about you." Richard intentionally employed a melodious, sympathetic tone. "Ma petite chou. You must have been terrified. But everything's okay now. All the bad stuff is over. You can come out."

The cat backed away, issuing a sustained hiss, and wedging her body into a narrow space between two steel water pipes. Richard reached forward, wanting to pet and reassure her. She spit a second warning, only this time louder and with far greater threat.

"Aw, no. You don't got to do that. It's just me," he told her. "Come here and I'll give you something to eat." He positioned himself within a few feet of the white cat. Blanche arched her back, fur spiked on end and her mouth contorted into an angry grimace as she growled another warning, this time lower and more guttural.

Richard moved forward, extending his hand palm up, to demonstrate that he meant her no harm. He assumed she'd be soothed by this gesture, but her response was to issue a piercing high-pitched cry. He hesitated, his heart pounding. Blanche had a fierce expression on her face: muscles taut, teeth exposed, lips drawn. Slowly, he stretched his fingers toward her, fluttering them a bit, and then remained completely still, expecting her to calm down, his hand inches from her chest.

With lightning speed Blanche sprang forward, emitting a terrifying scream while batting at him. Her sharp claws caught the fleshy part of Richard's right palm and shot across, tearing the skin, and then ripping it further as he reflexively pulled his hand away. Blood gushed to the surface. In spite of the pain, he managed to hold the cat by the scruff of the neck and wrap her in his tee-shirt, encircling her with his arms and restraining her against his chest. Blanche flailed, spit, and slashed wildly, shredding his shirt, cutting his chest, stomach, and forearms, and slicing deep into both hands as well as his fingers. Richard cried out, ultimately flinging the cat to the ground where she raced away, zigzag fashion, out of sight. He dropped to the ground, weeping. When his hands made contact with the dirt, it sent shock waves up his arms that shot up the sides of his neck and into his ears. He yowled like an injured coyote.

"Good Lord, Almighty!" Doreen shouted, drawn by the cat's cries and Richard's screams. He turned his head and saw her crawling under the house toward him. "What in God's name just happened?" she asked.

Richard raised his hands in the air. Dark red blood streamed down his forearms. Two deep gouges between the fingers of his right hand revealed bone and tendons. Doreen gasped. "Holy crap!" she said. "Come over here to me, child. Let's get you out from under here. We've got to clean those wounds up."

Richard followed, walking on his knees, barely able to keep thoughts together, his only consolation the hope that Doreen might have a mother's touch.

"Hold still, sugar." Doreen blotted Richard's wounds with a damp cloth, removing clumps of dirt as gingerly as possible. They sat at her kitchen table. His right hand was the more badly injured. She ignored her queasy stomach. The wounds were gruesome and there was quite a lot of blood. She'd had a little first aid training in a professional development course, but it dealt mostly with school playground accidents that called for soap and water, antiseptic wipes, splints, and cold compresses. "I'm thinking several of these might need a stitch or two," she said softly. "Roads might be clear enough to get you over to the—"

"No thanks," Richard interrupted. "I'll be okay."

Doreen shook her head. She knew better. "Your hands look mighty bad." She lifted his torn tee-shirt and dabbed the crisscross of surface cuts on his chest and belly with a couple of cotton balls soaked in hydrogen peroxide. He jumped when the cold liquid met his skin. "At the very least you ought to have that hand looked at," she said, referring to his right hand. "Some of those cuts are pretty darn nasty. Let me take you to the hospital. Come on. Let's give it a try."

"I appreciate it, but no. No, thanks."

Doreen shook her head as she raised a brown plastic bottle in her hand. "This may sting some, but you don't want an infection. Animal cuts are full of germs." She took hold of his right wrist. When hydrogen peroxide trickled over the worst slices in his hand, Richard cursed. Doreen didn't flinch. She held his wrist even more firmly and blew softly on the wounds as they gushed out bubbling white foam and streams of bright red blood. She applied a second round and held his torn skin together, taping the biggest cuts closed. She used the entire roll of gauze in her emergency kit. By the time she finished wrapping his right hand, it looked like he wore a boxing glove.

Richard inspected the bandage and rose from the chair. He swooned and staggered. Doreen jumped up to stand beside him, bracing him until he could steady himself. "Think I'll walk you home." She'd almost taken hold of his arm when she stopped. "Wait. I may still have a pill for pain somewhere. Got it last year for an abscessed tooth. I'm almost positive I had one left over." She avoided looking at the plaster board hanging from her ceiling as she reached into the kitchen cupboard, feeling around until her fingers found a pill container on the rear shelf. She placed the pill on Richard's tongue so he wouldn't have to use his wounded hands, and opened one of the water bottles she had purchased for the storm. He rolled his head back so she could pour a swallow into his mouth.

"How long until this thing starts working?" he asked.

She hunched her shoulders. "Let me drive you to the hospital," Doreen offered again. He shook his head and tried to smile.

As they arrived at her front door, he paused to collect himself. He noticed all the photographs that lined her entryway. "All of these family?" he asked. It just now occurred to him that he'd never been inside his neighbor's house before.

She raised her hands skyward. "And I praise the Lord for them, and for protecting my house and everything in it. Those pictures are my family's history. Would have been a terrible crime to lose them. Someday they'll belong to Curtis."

At that moment, a sudden and deafeningly loud percussive blast nearly knocked them over, slamming through the air with the force of dynamite, sending out shock waves like a bomb or sonic boom might. Doreen screamed. Richard stumbled. Photos fell from the wall, the glass inside one frame shattering when it struck the hardwood floor. Buddy yelped. "What the heck was that?" she asked stunned and trembling. Richard had rocked backwards against the front door, slamming it closed.

"Damn if I know," he answered shakily, hurting and off balance. "A transformer maybe?" She wrapped an arm around his waist and helped him stand upright.

"But the electricity's already out. How could a transformer explode like that?" She composed herself, opened her front door, and took a few cautious steps outside, expecting to see a rising plume of smoke or some other indication of an explosion, but saw nothing. She walked out onto the lawn and turned all the way around. "I don't get it," she said, cupping her hands behind her ears. "I don't hear anything at all." She returned to join Richard and Buddy, who were standing on her front stoop. "Whatever it was, it was mighty big."

Richard nodded. "Sure was." He yawned, his eyelids lowering to half-mast.

"Maybe that pain pill is starting to kick in. Come. Let's get you home." She took hold of his arm and led him forward, down her front steps.

Richard succumbed to another louder yawn. "Sorry. Don't mean to be rude. I haven't slept well in months. I could use a good rest."

"Hold on a sec." Doreen left Richard's side and dashed into her house. She returned, rummaging through her purse. "Ah ha." She pulled out a small white plastic bottle. "Bought these at the Rite-Aid, thinking I might need to take them during the storm. They're not prescription or anything. You might give one a try if you can't sleep." She pulled off the cap and spilled out two blue pills. "But I'm thinking that the pain pill should knock you out plenty good enough. I know it did me." Doreen slipped the sleeping pills into the pocket of

Richard's tee-shirt, put Buddy back in her house, told him to stay, and then helped Richard walk forward with her arm looped through his.

"You don't have to escort me home," he protested. "You need to sleep, too."

"You bet I do. But first we're going to get you safely inside your house." She guided him past the debris scattered across the lawn. "Hold on. Let me get the door for you." She reached for his doorknob. "Still think I should take you to get those cuts looked at." She pointed to a couple of red stains blossoming through the bright white gauze.

"Nah. I'll be all right. Go home," he said sleepily. "You've been great. I appreciate it. Now, get some rest yourself."

"Need me to help with anything inside?" she asked.

He shook his head. No one went into his house.

Doreen nodded wearily. She watched Richard step through his doorway; then she walked down onto the grass, pausing to shove several small, downed branches out of her path.

Richard pushed his front door closed, kicked off his shoes, and slid across the worn carpet in his stocking feet. He skated around the living room whistling *Ding, dong, the witch is*

dead. Doreen's pain pill had him loose. His right hand throbbed like a bass drum, but all other sensations were becoming thick and numb. A swell of relief lifted his spirits. The music's predictions had been wrong; his modest world hadn't been destroyed. Katrina hadn't caused him further loss, or the dreaded indignities of homelessness. Jubilant and grateful, he acknowledged his parents as he waltzed into the kitchen, thanking them for hearing his pleas, interceding, and protecting him. He swallowed both blue sleeping pills Doreen had given him using only the saliva in his mouth. Getting rest was important; it came so rarely. As he entered the bathroom, he saw his reflection in the medicine-chest mirror. He puckered his lips and threw himself a big kiss, catching a fleeting glimpse of that handsome young man once thought to have a future on the stage.

Richard felt better than he had in years. Free of obligation. Free of bodily burdens. Free, finally, to rest. He shut all the curtains in his house and scooted along in his stocking feet into his bedroom. After throwing a towel over his vomit on the floor, and vowing to clean it up later, he sat on the edge of his tousled bed, eager for the satisfaction and rejuvenation that sleep would bring him. Disregarding objections from his injured hands, he managed to peel off his socks and pull his torn and blood-streaked tee-shirt over his head. The scribble of claw marks on his chest, abdomen, and forearms shocked him. He admonished himself. *What was I thinking? Poor Blanche. She must have been totally traumatized.* He chuckled while wriggling out of his jeans, thinking he could win a hula-hoop contest. After brushing bits of grit from the bed sheets as best he could, he stretched out in his underwear and surrendered to exhaustion. His eyes closed and his breathing slowed.

For a time, he knew only blankness. The drugs kept him fully submerged. Not conscious of drawing breath; hardly conscious at all. Awareness floated somewhere far above him. Reaching it would have required far more energy than he could muster, so he simply let go and remained immersed, drifting into dreams of his mother. He saw her standing in front of him, her skin glowing tight and clear, and her hair hanging thick, dark, and straight like it had when she was young. He took her hand. They began to dance effortlessly and without words. When the music slowed, she drew nearer. Richard leaned forward, filled with eager anticipation. He could feel the warmth of her breath on his face. "Wait," she whispered in his ear. "It's not over."

Richard bolted upright in his bed, wide awake. He had no idea what his mother's words meant, but he knew they weren't good. He put on his eyeglasses and glanced around the room. Still leaden and blurry from the sleeping pills he'd taken, fresh grief flooded over him—the dream of his mother's visit clashing with the emptiness created by her absence. He leaned back, tearful, and took several shallow and labored breaths.

What's not over? he asked himself. He reached behind his head and parted the curtains above his headboard. Light entered the room and sparkled with unusual brightness; flickering and flitting, it cast odd dancing patterns on the walls and ceiling. Heavy and drowsy, he had no notion of how long he'd slept but knew that he wouldn't fall back asleep. He swiveled his legs over the bed and reached for his smokes. Before touching the pack, he lowered one foot onto the floor, but immediately jerked it up again. The floor felt wet. Without forethought, he reached down to confirm the improbable sensation and soaked his bandage. He shifted his eyeglasses, pushing them higher on the bridge of his nose and looked around the room. *What in the world?*

Water covered the bedroom floor—all of it. Puzzling. It made no sense. Could a pipe have broken? Had the toilet overflowed? Had he left a faucet running? Once out of bed, he sloshed through the standing water. It covered the entire hallway as well. Water came up to his ankles. He couldn't see anything running in the bathroom. He paused to listen but heard nothing. The world had gone strangely silent. He walked from the bathroom into the living room, moving the way a kid sloshes through puddles, splashing the water—but without a child's delight—creating ripples with every footstep. Miniature wakes lapped against the baseboards and rolled along the walls. Dreading what he would find outside, Richard closed his eyes before pushing the living-room curtains aside, their bottoms soaked and heavy. *This isn't over.* When he opened his eyes and looked out the window, he knew what his mother's warning had meant. A lake surrounded his house and extended throughout the neighborhood. *How could Gentilly Terrace flood? This area is higher than most of the city.*

It took him four tries to light a cigarette—his damaged hands dropping match after match into the water at his feet. What he saw was shockingly surreal. Everything as far as he could see had been transformed into a swamp, a bayou of houses instead of cypress trees emerging from the invading brown water. His playground as a child, and his entire universe as an adult, had been swallowed whole. Two doors down the street, the bright pink trim on Miss Phyllis' home remained as cheerful as ever, but the bricks at the water line had darkened and turned sullen. Unlike most other houses in this neighborhood, which stood on brick pilings, the Duplesis' house across the way had been built slab-on-grade. Being that much lower, it had fared far worse. Furniture floated inside its screened-in porch, a cushion bobbing on the dark water like a life preserver. A ninety-year-old widower who had raised five children on his own in that house, Frank Duplesis was terminally ill. Although he had been evacuated, Richard knew that the old man had wanted to die at home. That seemed unlikely now.

Splintered timbers from the Lagusi's demolished garage had formed logjams against the foundations of several neighboring houses. Most of his neighborhood's azaleas, elephant ears, and lilies had been swallowed by the floodwater. The crape myrtles lining the street appeared as flotsams of pink and green, the bases of their slender trunks obscured, submerged in the water's opaqueness. Repulsed yet mesmerized, the way one might react to seeing an accident, Richard found it impossible to look away until something he bumped with his foot got his attention. Submerged in the water on the floor was Saturday's newspaper, its headline warning, "Levees could be topped." *That's it!* The thunderous clap that nearly knocked Doreen and him off their feet was the sound of the man-made grass hills that formed levees bursting open. The levees bordering the London Street Canal were only a half-mile to the west, and those that held back the Industrial Canal were but a bit farther to the east.

Richard returned to his bedroom and dressed. He tried to roll up the bottom of his jeans, but his hands would not let him. Staccato puffs of cigarette smoke popped from his mouth as though from an antique railroad steam engine. He reentered the living room thinking that it couldn't be as bad as he'd thought—but it was. *Please God, let this be a nightmare!* It was no nightmare; it was really happening. Disbelief registered strongly, but reality did not yield in the slightest. The lowest row of his precious record albums was engulfed by the water. He rushed over to pull several from the bookcase, wiping soaked jackets on his tee-shirt before gently laying them on the sofa to dry. Vintage records in pristine condition damaged or destroyed. He knew heat ruined vinyl. Did water? It couldn't do them any good. And it surely would ruin their mint-condition jackets. Tchaikovsky, Verdi, Vivaldi, and Wagner were among the most apparent casualties, as he had arranged the albums in alphabetical order by composer, from top to bottom shelf. Overwhelmed by confusion and unsure what he should do, he walked in circles around the mahogany dining table and chairs that had belonged to his great-grandmother, the bottoms of their curved legs and claw feet completely immersed. His breathing rapid—a shallow, agitated pant.

Was it panic or did the water seem to be getting deeper? *Jesus God! The shoebox under my bed!* Richard cursed as he sloshed through the unwanted water and charged into his bedroom. Shoving aside his mother's half-submerged mattress, as well as floating bits of his stomach's earlier discharge, he got down on his knees. He soaked the bandage on his right hand the instant he reached under the bed to grab hold of the soggy cardboard box, which fell apart as he pulled on it, spilling most of its contents. Ignoring the physical distress these movements caused, he strained forward and swished his left hand around in the water until he fished up one of his mother's shoes. He also retrieved two scarves his mother had been fond of wearing and a pocket watch his father had received from management after working for the Hibernia Bank for twenty-five years.

Having no idea how much higher the water might get, he bundled these and other found treasures in the bottom of his shirt and headed for the attic. The staircase he'd pulled down earlier still hung from the hall ceiling. But, as he started to climb, holding onto the rungs with his less injured hand, his mother's hairbrush, which held precious strands of her gray hair, slipped from his clumsy gauze-wrapped hand, and fell into the water. Richard shrieked as he watched it sink and disappear. After putting the other souvenirs in the attic, he descended the ladder and searched in the murky water until he found the brush. On the verge of tears, he cheered and clasped it to his chest before climbing the steps again and setting it in the furnace-like heat of the attic. After that, he stashed all but one of his remaining packs of cigarettes and a frayed blue cotton blanket up there as well.

Astounded by the speed at which the floodwater continued to rise, Richard sought to sharpen his focus. He waded through the now knee-deep water and, despite its increasing resistance, returned to the living room. Knowing that he couldn't carry all his many vinyl recordings into the attic, he selected a most cherished few—those featuring Maria Callas—and put them on top of the tall china hutch in the dining room. They were high above the water, but were they high enough? As the unknowns mounted, and the futility of this effort became more apparent, his spirit darkened further. Katrina's wind and rain may have done little damage to the house, but this flood would destroy everything, and he had no flood insurance.

In a tizzy, he splashed from one room to the next without any idea of what he should do. He witnessed the rising water carry off objects—a flotilla of syringes and rubber gloves that he'd used when caring for his mother; stubbed out cigarette butts from the ashtray on the coffee table; a few empty soda cans he had not bothered to throw away. Every time he pushed forward to take hold of something, the ripples he created on the water sent the object farther out of reach.

Adrenalin masked all but the sharpest pain produced by his injuries. He cupped the invading water in his hands and brought it to his nose. It smelled brackish, but beyond that he detected no odor. *The carpets will dry. And maybe the water will drain before the floors and walls warp too badly.* He wondered if the generators at the city's pumping stations still functioned. Though clearly overwhelmed, they might push the water out soon enough. Of course, the pumps required electricity to operate. As he shifted his attention from inside to out, he caught sight of a small creature swimming frantically on top of the water. At first glance, he thought it might be Blanche, drenched, but then recognized that it was a rat in a dash for dry ground. Sickened and frightened, Richard climbed atop his mother's hospital bed frame and, ignoring the searing pain it caused, curled his tall body into the fetal position on its bare metal mesh.

Water in every corner of her house! It conspired with the intensifying heat and humidity to make the mere act of breathing necessarily deliberate and effortful. Moisture beaded on all the walls and dripped from the ceilings, peeling the edges of her wallpaper, and fogging every window and mirror. Doreen consciously pulled the heavy air into her lungs and then pushed it out with her mouth hanging open. She picked up a magazine and fanned her reddened face.

"Hotter 'n Hades," her father used to say. To beat Louisiana's grueling summer heat, he would sometimes take the family for Sno-Balls at one of the many stands throughout the city. No matter where they went, Doreen would always order cherry. She liked the color best and was contemptuous of her sisters for choosing such unappealing flavors as lime, which was an unnatural green, or coconut, which was clear. Sometimes her parents would let their daughters go the extra mile and top their cones of shaved ice with drizzles of sweetened condensed milk. The chilly treat sounded like ambrosia to her now. She thought of how, because they'd had no air conditioning back then, her family went to Lincoln Beach on the hottest days, which was the section of Lake Pontchartrain's shoreline where blacks had been allowed to bathe. She remembered the fun she'd had playing there with her sisters, and how much they liked to stand with the lake water up around their knees, cooling off while squishing the bottom muck between their toes.

Lake water! She found nothing fun or refreshing about having it inundate her living room, although Buddy seemed to enjoy it. He played in the water gleefully, splashing and paddling around the room. Now and then, Doreen could hear Richard cursing from across the way, his dismay completely understandable. With so many worries of her own, she had no comforting words to offer. She stared with resignation at the grimy bathtub-like ring deposited on her walls, a foot or so above the baseboards. Seeing that filmy ring meant the water would have dropped below its highest level. "It's going down!" she cheered aloud.

"Hey, Richard!" she yelled across their common driveway, now transformed into a canal. "You hoo! Richard? Can you hear me?" Sweat cascaded down the sides of her face as she eagerly called out to share the good news.

He didn't answer. She heard him cursing furiously.

"I know, sugar. Horrible, isn't it? Everything's getting ruined. And I refinished these floors myself." She mopped her forehead and neck with a folded paper towel. "Spent two whole weeks on my hands and knees sanding them."

Richard stopped yelling.

Doreen wiped her runny nose. "Crazy thing is," she shouted, "I never heard anything. When I saw the water coming in, I ran around with towels, trying to sop it up." She had no idea whether Richard could hear her but didn't care. "Can't believe how hot it's gotten! Worse than a steam bath!" She peeled her blouse from her chest and shook it. "I've got plenty of food and water over here, but you'll have to come over to get some. I'm not going out in all this water. Bad enough having it come inside my house." Her desperate desire to escape was thwarted by knowing that the water outside her elevated house was several feet deeper.

Doreen sat in her living room on a damp sticky chair, completely dejected. No way would Curtis be returning home on Monday now. She lowered her head into her hands and gazed at her toes, which had turned a sickly beige color. She lifted her water-wrinkled feet onto the seat of the chair. Overcome by heat and exhausted by a tidal wave of emotions that oppressed her, it wasn't long before she struggled to keep her eyes open. That is until she heard several thumps coming from her front door. *Richard?* Doreen shook her head vigorously in response to the sound of several more loud bumps. She moved through the water, approached the door, and reached for the knob. Hesitant, she decided it might be wise to check outside first. Though she couldn't see anything when she looked out of her window, she definitely heard the bumping sound again. Something knocked against her door. *Oh, Lord! What if it's snakes?* The possibility of snakes slithering around her house pushed her toward hysteria. Instead of opening the door Doreen leaned against it with all her might to keep it closed; the water had started rising once again, faster than it had before.

She told herself to remain calm and develop a plan, figure out a route of escape. That meant cracking open the front door to have a look around but, as soon as she did, water rushed in. As she pushed the door closed, something rough and slimy rubbed against her leg. A shiver ran down her spine. Had she just shut something *inside* the house? She felt it again and screamed like the victim in a horror movie, springing backwards and falling on her bottom in the water. Near panic, she flailed, her body creating waves that ricocheted off the wall and rolled over her shoulders from behind. Nearly undone, she flipped over, used her hands to climb the wall and stand, the weight of her wet clothes making her movements more difficult. The mysterious creature that had touched her leg wriggled closer. *Sweet Jesus!* she sighed, relieved that it was not a snake, but dismayed that it was a fish. A fish had actually made its way down her street and was now swimming inside her house! She opened her door and pushed the silvery thing with the side of her foot, sending it zipping outside, across her front stoop, its dorsal fin lying flat against its body. "No you don't!" she yelled when it turned around and careened toward the house once again.

A second fish smacked against her outside stair railing and headed for the house. "Hell, no! You keep out of here!" she shouted, blocking the fish from entering her doorway as though a soccer goalie. Suddenly, there were several more, sending her into retreat. It was then that she noticed tiny whirlpools and small ripples on the water's surface—evidence of a current, like in a river. *Please God. Let the pumps be working. Let the water be draining.*

After managing to push her front door shut, she got herself to the kitchen, shoving Buddy, who swam beside her, on top of the kitchen counter, his nails clicking on the laminate. She pulled a small Styrofoam cooler from her broom closet thinking she might need to cling to it for flotation if, instead of draining, the water continued to rise.

Mired in defeat and surrender, Richard's eyes fixed on the black bobby pin he held between his fingers as water rose around him. This bobby pin had belonged to Charmaine Evans. Thoughts of Charmaine Evans offered no escape from things unpleasant.

Fifty-ish, graying and sturdy, Nurse Evans was an African American woman with a confident middle-aged physique, soft handsome features, and a reassuring smile. But she was no angel. She was a cold-blooded killer. She'd done it and he'd seen her. It was with great reluctance that Richard had allowed the doctors to admit his mother to the hospital when she began to have trouble breathing. He didn't trust doctors *or* hospitals. Just two days after that, when he'd stepped outside briefly for a smoke break, he'd walked in on Nurse Evans holding an empty syringe while his mother convulsed and struggled. Did Nurse Evans panic? No. Did she seem concerned? Not even a little. Richard caught her smile as she whispered, "It's okay. Go if you want. Sleep tight."

Damn her! It was not okay! The bitter taste of bile filled his mouth. What gall! Pretending to care; claiming good motives! He had spent fourteen years doing whatever was required to keep his mother alive—feeding her, bathing her and, after she had deteriorated further, even manually moving her bowels—and in a matter of moments, Charmaine Evans had simply invited death in. To Richard, she had committed murder. He wished he could squeeze her neck just like he squeezed the bobby pin that had once been in Nurse Evans' hair.

Doreen's pleas from next door barely penetrated his angry stupor. He'd heard her but she sounded remote, abstract. Richard stood and rubbed his eyes, awakening from his trance to find even more water had invaded his living room. He pushed his way to the open side window and called out, "Hey, Doreen! You okay?"

Her face filled the window frame, her expression frantic, her face contorted by panic. "No! Help me! Please! I need your help!"

"Okay, I'm coming." Richard fought his way to the front of his house and outside to his stoop, water wrapping around his thighs. As he pushed against its resistance, he realized the effort it would take to get from his place to hers. Down his front steps the water would be deeper, and he had no idea what obstacles might lay hidden beneath its dark surface.

A foul smell, like that of sewage, had entered the air. He told himself to ignore it and continue, shivering as he sank up to his stomach. He moved forward through oily slicks riding atop, while sliding his feet along the ground, working not to fall or stumble over unseen hazards lurking below. The water itself didn't feel particularly cool or warm, just greasy, dirty, and very, very wrong.

Though his bandages were already wet, he kept his right hand in the air so that the cuts Blanche had inflicted would not touch the polluted water, and he held his nose with his left, breathing through his mouth as he continued. The water's buoyancy made him feel lighter than he'd expected but, when he reached Doreen's front landing and climbed out of the deepest water, his wet clothing weighed him down.

He tried to open her door with his injured hands but couldn't and wound up pounding on it several times with his elbow. Forcing the door open required both of their efforts. "Thank you, sweet Jesus!" she cried, glassy-eyed, her complexion sickly. She pointed to her kitchen and to Buddy, and then latched hold of Richard's forearm. "I can't—" Doreen stopped. Her green eyes grew wider and unblinking. "Oh, dear God! Water's coming up even faster now! How can this be happening? I don't understand." She pointed to the doily on her dining tabletop as it floated away.

Before she could say another word, the bleating of a car's horn cut through the air. Doreen stumbled. Buddy jumped down and swam toward her as she came up flailing and spitting.

Without a thought for his injuries, Richard took hold of the dog's neck with one hand and used the other to help Doreen. After getting Doreen upright and putting her hand around Buddy's collar so that she could hold him, Richard looked outside to assess. An empty parked car on their street had started on its own. *How is that possible?* Richard heard its motor chug, trying to turn over, and saw its lights flashing on and off. The horn registered the auto's improbable protest: a mechanical cry for help. Moments later the car went silent, as though drowned. Doreen and Buddy joined him in her doorway, all eyes fixed in amazement.

Richard turned toward her. "Where's your attic?"

She shook her head.

"Okay. We'll go to my house. Who knows how high the water will get before this is over." He couldn't believe he'd just offered to bring Doreen into his house. The words had leaped out of his mouth.

"To your house? But how?" Her voice strained and cracking with anxiety.

"It's only water. You're already wet. If it gets too deep, we'll swim."

"No! You don't understand! I can't swim."

Richard saw embarrassment beneath her fear, and even at such a turbulent moment found her vulnerability compelling. "Okay," he said, turning around. "Take hold of me. I'm taller than the deepest water we'll go through. As long as you hold on, you won't have to swim."

"Bless you," she said, breathlessly.

"Get on my back, wrap your legs around my waist, and hold on tight," he told her. He watched her check the buttons on her blouse, making sure they were fastened.

"Hope you can hold me. I've let myself get so fat," she whispered, hanging her head as she clamped onto his body. He threaded his arms under her legs and started to inch forward.

"No! Wait!" she cried, arching her body backwards. "My baby's picture book!"

The last thing Richard wanted to do now was stop. He worried about losing his resolve. He wanted this ordeal to be over as quickly as possible, but when Doreen grew rigid, he yielded to her determination. "Okay. Go ahead."

She climbed down.

"It's going to be hard enough carrying you and leading Buddy," he warned. "I don't know how many of those pictures I can actually hold."

Doreen shook her head. "Not the framed ones. My baby's picture book." Doreen waved for Richard to help her into Curtis's bedroom, where they pushed past the bed, which was already under water. She struggled to reach a blue leather album on the top shelf of his bookcase. When Richard raised his arm to get it for her, she yelled an emphatic, "No! Don't touch it!" She climbed on top of her son's desk.

Hugging it and whimpering with gratitude, Doreen again took hold of Richard from behind as if getting a horsy ride, squeezed the photo album between the two of them, and put her forehead on his shoulder. She shivered and shut her eyes.

Her breasts pressed softly against his back, and the heat from her legs warmed his rib cage as they wrapped firmly around him. His cut hands held her inner thighs. Her diaphragm expanded and contracted. He was aware of all this as her chest and stomach convulsed slightly with her sobs. He felt ashamed that he noticed the various intimacies of this moment under circumstances like this, but he did. *I'm so venal,* he thought, *so thoroughly corrupt.*

He pushed forward with her body curled around his. The two approached her front door, moving through the entry hall where her family photos hung. Several had fallen off the wall and into the water; others remaining on the wall were below the waterline. She opened her eyes and moaned with despair. As they approached the open doorway, Doreen grunted and leaned backward, trying to take hold of her front doorknob. "Please," she pleaded, "I know it's crazy, but I can't leave my house open like this."

Richard stopped. He understood. Buddy continued past, paddling outside of the house. Richard backed up, placing Doreen within reach of her door. She tried but couldn't pull it closed on her own. With searing effort, he supported her bottom from underneath with his right arm and injured hand, while taking hold of the door and pulling with his left. Accomplishing the task required their combined strength.

"Bless you, again," Doreen said as she tucked her head against his shoulder and closed her eyes once more.

To his great relief her body grew lighter as they descended into higher water, although, as the water rose, her grip on him clamped down tighter. Buddy snorted as he swam beside them. Richard made certain to keep his lips closed firmly to prevent dirty water from accidentally getting into his mouth. His mind ran through all the chemicals and fertilizers, rodents and insects, feces and garbage the water carried, and that they themselves were immersed in. Between here and the levees were cemeteries, gas stations, dumpsters, and refuse heaps. He gagged at the thought—and the smell, as the stench of sewage lines that had regurgitated their contents grew more pronounced.

He shuffled forward, making each movement with caution and care, praying that the water's buoyancy would keep Doreen's weight from becoming too much of a strain. All they needed now was for his back to spasm or go out. *If that happens, we're both as good as drowned.*

Planks of wood, once part of the Lagusi's garage, drifted past, some with splintered ends. Nails stuck out of others, like some crude weapon. Even destroyed, that place remained dangerous. He tried not to think about the open wounds on his submerged hands, or give the burning sensation that plagued his palms much attention. "Doing all right?" he asked Doreen.

She let loose a bitter-edged laugh.

"What?" he said as they reached the stairs to his house. What could possibly be funny about standing chest deep in foul water? he wondered.

"And I was worried about *my floors*."

Once inside his house, Doreen climbed down from Richard's back. Water lapped at her armpits. She stood on tiptoe with her neck stretched, holding onto Buddy's collar with one hand and her son's photo album above her head in the other. The album dripped water, having been under the surface while going between the two houses. Richard headed toward the attic stairs. "Wait! Don't leave me!" she cried.

Richard turned. His neighbor looked like a plump Statue of Liberty holding a wet torch; only instead of inspirational, she looked terrified—the light in her eyes doused and her forehead rippled with fear.

"We can stay down here and stand on chairs if you want. See how deep the water gets. Or go into the attic. The attic's right up there." Richard pointed. "Your choice. But I'll warn you, it's really, really hot up there."

Doreen pointed at the attic stairs, gave him a thumb's up, and then waved for him to come back and get her. "At least it's dry up there."

"For now," he replied sardonically, approaching her with his arms extended.

"If the water gets as high as your attic," she said and burst into tears, "you might as well kiss my ass goodbye."

Richard shook his head and took her hand. "Goddamn bastards. They knew this would happen one day. None of them cared enough to protect us."

"Who knew? Who are you talking about?"

"The Corps of Engineers, the Levee Board, Orleans Parish, the State, the Feds—all of them. They were supposed to protect us. Anyone with half a brain could see that the levees were in terrible shape." He scoffed. "They all knew. I'm sure that the cannon-like sound we heard, that big kaboom, was one of the levee walls busting open. Other levees probably have come down, too—a chain reaction. Most are just built-up mud hills with grass growing on them. Many were already leaking before the hurricane." Richard placed her hand on an attic stair rung. "If the water's this deep in Gentilly," he said, "I can only imagine what everywhere else is like. The entire city must be under water."

"The entire city . . ." she repeated, her voice trailing off. "Superdome, too?"

Richard nodded; his expression intended to convey empathy.

She shook her head, the prospect unimaginable. "Can't be."

Richard frowned and tilted his head from one side to the other, but said nothing.

"You're wrong. You've got to be wrong." She turned and climbed the steep stairs, crawling through the rectangular opening in the hallway ceiling. "Oooweee," she yelled when a full blast of the attic heat hit her. "You certainly weren't wrong about it being really really hot up here. At least the picture book should dry."

"Like I said, we can wait and see how much higher the water will get."

"No, siree," she called back to him. "It's way high enough for me already!"

Richard looked up from the bottom of the ladder. "Hey. Come back here, will you? You forgot something."

Doreen poked her head through the hatch, a quizzical expression on her face. Richard pointed at the dog. She smacked her forehead. "Come," she called emphatically, trying to command the dog to climb the ladder. Confusion registered on Buddy's face. Doreen lowered herself down several steps, wrapped her hand around his collar, and began pulling him from above.

Though Buddy now seemed to understand where she wanted him to go, he was too frightened to do it. And since his weight and slick wet coat made lifting him up impossible, Richard had to join in the effort. He pushed the dog from behind as she pulled from above, until the dog finally managed to scramble up and through the opening and into the attic.

Richard winced, the stinging pain in his hands and fingers excruciating. It was the main reason that exhaustion hadn't overtaken him. He heard Buddy shaking the water from his coat. "I'm going to gather a few things," he called to Doreen. "Watch for me. I'll hand them up to you."

"Okay." Doreen soothed Buddy by rubbing him on the chest. "Good boy," she told him, exhaustion in her voice.

Richard knew that his cuts had opened while carrying Doreen and shoving the dog up the stairs. His right hand felt on fire. The gauze and tape were a sopping and bloody mess.

He swiveled through chest-deep water, pushing past several faded silk flowers that had been part of an arrangement in the living room, now floating above his mother's submerged hospital bed as though ceremonially strewn. Some of the rubber gloves he'd used while tending her bobbed on top of the water like jellyfish. Across the room, four golden spires protruded from the water like miniature navigational markers. He recognized them as belonging to an anniversary clock that sat on top of his long-broken console television.

In a dither and unsure what to salvage, he looked around, surveying in every direction. Oily water obscured nearly everything below the windowsills, making invisible threats out of the books and newspapers that lay, heavy as rocks, on the floor. His cherished turntable, amplifier, and speakers were submerged. He diverted his attention from them by reaching for the albums he'd placed on top of the dining hutch, carrying them to the steps, and calling for Doreen. When he handed them to her, he heard her annoyance crackle.

"What'll we do with these? We need drinking water—and food!" Her voice snapped with urgency as she set the albums on the attic floor.

Nodding quietly, Richard pushed his way into the kitchen. He gathered four small jars of water that he'd filled before the storm and tucked them under his arm. He didn't see much else of use—but also took a nearly empty jar of peanut butter and a half bottle of vodka that had been his mother's before Alzheimer's took her away. He called out for Doreen, who scurried partway down the ladder, nodding when he handed her the jars of drinking water.

"Anything more?" she asked, seeing how small the jars were. "These will be gone in half an hour."

"How about this?" Richard said, passing her the vodka.

"Great! Now we won't have to miss out on cocktail hour! Got olives?" She scoffed. "Honestly, we need a whole lot more food and water. What about the stew I gave you? And there's a ton of food sitting over at my place. Plenty of water, too. It's all right there, in my kitchen."

"I couldn't make it."

"Please," she pleaded, "get anything you can. We could be stuck here overnight."

Richard shook his head and pushed through the water, returning to the kitchen, but other than finding a few canned items, the pantry was empty. Since cans are watertight, he figured he could come back and get them later, after resting.

He hesitated in front of the refrigerator because he knew pulling on the handle would hurt. Just grasping it stung.

Opening the door required several attempts. When he finally succeeded, the filthy water surged forward, scooping up all but the few things he'd put on the top shelf. Since he hadn't put the lid on the container with the remainder of Doreen's shrimp stew, it was immediately swamped by floodwater. A nearly empty mayonnaise jar, a cup of apple sauce, and a decomposing head of lettuce floated away. The butter dish and a bag holding something he couldn't identify sank out of sight. He caught two cans of Diet Coke with his better hand before they could go under, and retrieved a small plastic container with some spaghetti and tomato gravy that had long overstayed its welcome. Brown water had contaminated everything else.

"You got us something to eat," Doreen said with a smile, receiving the food from his dirty, torn hands.

He pointed to the container holding spaghetti. "Don't know. It's pretty old."

"Where's the shrimp stew I gave you?"

"Sunk."

"We'll need more stuff. Especially water. It's so hot up here."

"Don't think there is more water."

"Check. Please. Anything, anything at all to drink!"

Richard forced his way back into the kitchen. The flood-water was continuing to rise. His leg muscles quivered and shook; his left calf cramped. He knew this would have to be his last trip. There was no more drinking water, and so he returned with the only thing he could find—an unopened jar of grape jelly. "Here, take this," he said, handing it to her. "I've got to quit. I'm coming up." His leg muscles were fluttering badly; he didn't know if he could climb the ladder. He backed down into the water and took a couple of labored breaths while calling upon his resolve. Before making another attempt, he pulled a picture off the wall.

"Take this from me, will you?" he asked as he took a final look around. Feeling lightheaded, and with dark spots encroaching upon his field of vision, he fought to keep from blacking out. He knew if he let that happen, he would sink under the water, and she couldn't help him.

Doreen held Richard under his arms, guiding his six-foot-two frame up the last stairs and into the stale attic air. Tremors coursed through his body. It had to be at least 110 degrees in the confined sweltering space, yet he shook as though freezing. He had a frightening hollow pallor, like that of a ghost.

She set him on the floor. He sat with his legs straight out and arms folded over his lap. Ever so lightly, she laid a hand on his shoulders, expecting a protest. When there was none, she began to massage his back gently. The contours of his clinging wet tee-shirt revealed ridge lines of seized, knotted muscles.

"I've got to lie down," he murmured.

"Sure, sugar. Let's get you over to where you can ..."

He flopped backwards, nearly unconscious. Doreen caught him just before his head hit, lowering him the rest of the way onto the rough attic floor. From there he rolled onto his side, drawing his legs up toward his chest. His eyes remained closed. Within seconds his breathing slowed, though his body continued to shake spasmodically. She reached over and removed his eyeglasses.

Stillness contrasted with the hectic, frenetic turbulence of their forced retreat into this cramped and airless space. Beyond the whistle of Richard's light snore, Buddy's snuffling, and the pounding of her own agitated heartbeat, Doreen heard nothing—no sounds at all—not wind, nor rain, nor traffic, nor sirens, not even birds. Except for a thin shaft of light in a corner, daylight entered the windowless attic through a louvered, triangularly shaped air vent in the attic wall. Stacks of books and boxes, bundled magazines, shopping bags, broken furniture, and old toys occupied most of the floor. The sloped ceiling made the tight space feel that much smaller. The unfinished walls, splintery floor, exposed rafters and joists, and threads of electrical wiring impeded movement. Most were coated with dust and cobwebs. Years of accumulated mold and mustiness caught in her sinuses and the back of her throat. Doreen tried shutting her eyes, but every place she put herself, physically and emotionally, felt hard and uncomfortable. Simply sitting in this place demanded effort. Wet clothes added to her discomfort. She desperately wanted to shower. Her hair had absorbed foul odors and a crusty residue of grit and filth caked on her skin. Buddy added a strong smell of wet dog to the mix. But nothing competed with the needle-like prickling effects of the heat.

Occasionally, she shuffled sideways to peer into Richard's house through the attic hatch. She thought the water's rise might have slowed. When she wasn't asking God to make it recede, she was reprimanding herself for never having learned to swim. She returned to sit near Richard, who was now unresponsive. "Ah, ah, bay-bee," she sang, the nonsense lullaby one she'd sung to her son when an infant. *How will Curtis get home to me now, through all this disgusting water?*

She thanked God that her parents and sisters had taken refuge in the Superdome, rather than at her house. Certainly, they would have the benefit of city services, health care, and protection, presuming of course that Richard was wrong, that the stadium had remained dry. Her folks were old and unwell. Her mother suffered from advanced diabetes and her father had a weak heart. Her younger sisters might be with them, but neither of them had ever shown much resourcefulness.

What if Mama didn't bring enough insulin? A host of bad thoughts interrupted her prayers. *What if Daddy's heart can't take the strain? What if people stampede for the exits?* She glanced over at Richard, his breathing deep and low. "Ah, ah, bay-bee," she sang as she worked to calm herself and prevent her imagination from manufacturing a hundred more un-happy scenarios. The smell of sweat merged with the stench coming from her fouled clothes and the dog, odors impossible to ignore. She checked the level of the putrid water down-stairs every so often. *How close is it to reaching the attic now?*

Every terrible, terrifying image lingered. And she'd thought time moved slowly before! She sought distraction as she continued to sing, at first petting Buddy, and then taking stock of their shadowy surroundings, catching sight of several old boxes illuminated in the half-light. She recognized the names, D.H. Holmes and Maison Blanche, local department stores that had long since gone out of business. Their boxes had become coveted souvenirs—her mother had a couple stashed away. Doreen wondered what treasures they might harbor—vintage clothes, beaded handbags, elbow-length gloves, old hats? She was tempted to open them, if for no other reason than to pass the time but was hesitant to violate Richard's privacy.

She could only shake her head when she spotted the recordings Richard had saved from downstairs leaning against a wall. Opera records, all featuring the same singer—Maria Callas. *That lady must be pretty damn good if they were the first things he thought to protect.* Beyond the records and old boxes, she saw a miniature train set constructed on several sections of plywood that had been pieced together. Narrow tracks carried a bright red engine and six cars through a little town and a forest of tiny trees. The set looked practically new. *Wouldn't Curtis love this? Oh, Curtis!* Thoughts of him returned. Tears spilled. How long until they would be together again?

Doreen picked up the framed picture Richard had rescued at the last minute. Through watery eyes, she inspected the photograph of a young girl sporting a pixie haircut, with bangs hanging over her forehead and past her eyebrows. The squared-off hairstyle, sideways glance, and devilish grin reminded Doreen of flappers from the 1920s. She turned over the frame. "Thelma (Dookie) Gautier, age 14." Richard's mother. So, this was the young girl who would give Richard life, and during her long years of illness slowly drain it away.

During the past three weeks, while Curtis had been at summer camp, Doreen suffered glimpses of her own compulsion to latch onto her son for companionship. While intellectually she knew how wrong that was, emotionally she understood how such things happen. She could only imagine how widowhood and the dread that comes with advancing illness might have compounded this compelling desire.

Buddy moaned as he walked over and lowered himself beside her on the attic floor. He seemed comforted when she began to pet him once again. *So hot,* she thought, *and he's wearing a fur coat.*

"Ah, ah, bay-bee." Doreen's attention shifted from the dog to the man lying on the other side of where she sat. He'd become more than someone who lived on her block—more than the quirky, disaffected personality that Markita thought deranged and possibly dangerous—but the man who had saved her from drowning and who had carried her on his back to safety. Was he a gentle wounded soul driven to eccentricity by isolation, or a seething homicidal pervert like that guy in *Psycho*, as Markita had warned? All Doreen knew for certain was that he had protected her from the rising water.

Thirst interrupted her thoughts and scattered her focus. Heat this intense had depleted and dehydrated her. Richard had only salvaged four little jelly jars of water, two cans of Diet Coke, and a half bottle of vodka. She opened one of the jars and held it to her lips. Though she took only a few small sips, she drained the jar of nearly one-third of its contents. She swished the water throughout her mouth to get its full benefit before swallowing, slowly. It soothed the rawness in her mouth and throat momentarily but went down too fast to extinguish it.

She stood, bent slightly at the waist, her head narrowly avoiding a beam, and looked around to assess her surroundings. She could see no route out other than the stairs that dropped to the flooded main floor of Richard's house. Even the slats in the wall's vent, which provided the only source of light and fresh air, were fixed in place. She could do little more than stick her fingers between their narrow openings.

Doreen returned to the open hatch, laid down on her belly, and leaned over to check the water level, lowering her arm down as far as she could. The tips of her fingers brushed the water's surface. It had to be at least six feet deep or more. Lord! Everything had happened so fast! Desperation clutched her by the throat. Held captive by floodwaters below, a roof above, and attic walls all around, she could see no escape.

Every joint in his stiff and brittle body pressed against the unforgiving floor, but it was his back that complained loudest. Swinging between consciousness and delirium, he struggled to embrace the pain—an all-too-familiar exhortation throughout his life.

Fever ignited vivid dreams, removing him from the confines of the attic where he and Doreen had sought refuge from the flooding. One dream sent him back in time to when he was a young man, when his fear and shame had been overtaken by desire; to the evening when he had borrowed his parents' car and driven alone to the French Quarter, compelled to find a place he'd heard spoken of only in whispers and snide remarks. He'd wandered the narrow streets with no more than a vague notion of where to go, moving through raucous crowds of tourists and locals with his head down, wanting to avoid notice, assuming his motives were transparent. He'd been taught that such urges were wicked. He'd asked God to take these urges away, but they'd only grown more insistent.

His vision of the peach-colored building located toward the upper end of Bourbon Street was as tangible to him now as the attic had been earlier. On that first outing so long ago, he had recognized this bar as the place he was looking for when he saw its rowdy, mostly male clientele overflowing onto the street from swinging double doors. A few steps inside, a single gas flame flickered in an open metal cage, its soft light intended to flatter the men's faces. He'd entered the building haltingly, arms held tightly at his side. He'd weaved hesitantly through the packed space and clouds of blue cigarette smoke to stand against a dark brick wall. Conversations and laughter rolled over the top of reverberant dance music. The men surrounding him held and hugged one another openly. He watched with odd discomfort, and yet to see men behave in this manner felt strangely reassuring. He could not stop staring. For years he'd felt separate, different; he found it hard to believe that in this place he was but one soul in a crowd.

Innately cautious and wary, Richard avoided even the most casual of contact in the dense crush, enforcing a physical barrier by folding his arms across his chest. That worked until a heavy-set older man chose to ignore Richard's protective stance. The man's watery bloodshot eyes, unpleasant smell of alcohol, and protruding stomach moved uncomfortably close. Startled, Richard didn't know how to respond. He simply turned his head and shifted his stance to create a bit more distance between them.

"Larry," the man said, holding out a pale, pudgy hand.

"No," Richard replied.

"No. It's *my* name." He chuckled. "Don't be scared. I won't bite." He smiled. His words slurred as much by alcohol as by his syrupy Mississippi drawl.

Richard wanted to run but his feet felt glued to the floor. He pivoted slightly without offering his name in return or shaking the man's hand.

"Can I buy you a drink?" The man pressed closer.

"No thanks," Richard replied. He didn't want to talk to anyone. He'd only wanted to look around.

"What's the matter, handsome? Don't you drink?"

"No, I don't." The words sounded choked by his constricted windpipe.

The man slipped a stubby hand around Richard's waist and pulled him closer still. "How about a dance then? You like to dance, don't you?" Richard had no idea how to respond, or what the man might do next.

"S'cuse me," Richard heard someone say assertively. A short young man with a ruddy complexion, reddish hair, freckled face, and stick-out ears smiled as he insinuated himself between the two of them. "Here's that drink you asked me for, heart." He gave a glass to Richard and pushed forward, forcing the older man's hand from Richard's waist. "Hey, I asked politely this time. I said excuse me. Now shoo. Go away. Leave me and my boyfriend alone."

Confusion registered on the older man's face, along with doubt. He glared, gave Richard a sneering grimace and, without saying another word, disappeared into the crowd.

Richard waited a moment and then tried to return the young man's drink. "Thanks for that," he said in a manner he hoped would convey his gratitude.

"No problem. It's only Pop Rouge."

"No. I mean for helping me out."

"Oh! Sure. Old guys hit on me, too. It's no fun." The young man leaned against the wall. His deep blue eyes drilled with intensity, while ears sticking out from behind his copper-colored hair added an unexpected whimsical dimension. "I'm René Kilpatrick."

"Richard Girard." They shook hands.

"Richard? Don't imagine people call you Dick, do they? Not a good nickname for a homo."

Richard didn't know how to reply. He'd never heard such a cavalier use of the word "homo."

"No offense. After all—everyone thinks René is a girl's name."

"I don't. It's French."

"So I'm told, but I'm from the Irish Channel and there it's a girl's name. I don't have a drop of French blood in me. My mother just liked the name." He rolled his eyes.

"As if being queer isn't hard enough, she had to saddle me with a girl's name to top it off."

René's mischievous smile and self-deprecating humor appealed and put Richard at ease. He smiled in reply. "It's my first time here."

"I only started coming a couple weeks ago myself." René leaned close and whispered. "I won't be eighteen for another two months. Most bars don't card you unless you push your luck. That's why I only order soft drinks. They never ask for ID." He paused. "How old are you?"

"Almost twenty." Richard lit a cigarette and looked hesitantly at René, not knowing whether to offer him one or not.

"No, thanks. I don't smoke. In fact, I have to step out of here sometimes cause the smoke gets to me. Allergies."

"Sorry." Richard pulled the cigarette from his lips and rolled it between his fingers to dislodge the burning tobacco, saving the remainder.

René waved his hand through the smoke that pervaded the bar. "Don't bother. But let's get out of here. Want to walk outside for a minute?"

Richard followed René through the crowd and out the swinging double doors. A fog created by dense New Orleans humidity slid over them, replacing the cigarette smoke. René pulled a piece of folded paper from his shirt pocket and held it out for Richard to take. "It's my phone number. Call me the next time you go to the bar. Maybe we could meet and go together. You know, for protection."

"Yeah, sure," Richard replied. He read the number. It was an uptown exchange. He refolded the paper and placed it in his wallet.

"What now?" René asked. "You going back inside?"

"No. I should get home. I've got my parents' car."

"Where'd you park?"

"Over on Rampart."

"Me too. Mind if I walk with you?"

"Course not." Richard welcomed his company.

Streetlight revealed René to be every bit as young as he'd said, and perhaps younger. Richard could tell that René liked him; he saw it in his attentive, overly eager demeanor. He liked René, too, but not in that way. *We'll be friends,* Richard thought.

As the two approached the broader and more brightly lit Rampart Street, René reached over and took Richard's hand. Richard instinctively withdrew, but then relented. The overt gesture made him uncomfortable, but it seemed harmless enough, especially considering René's earlier assistance. "That's another gay bar," René said, pointing. The two slowed as they approached a three-story brick building with tall narrow doors painted glossy black. Music pounded from inside. "There are lots of them in the Quarter."

Richard wanted to remember where these bars were, amazed that a whole new world of possibilities existed. He examined the building's façade, unaware of tires squealing behind them. He did remember hearing someone yell, "Faggots," right before something slammed into the small of his back so hard that it knocked him off his feet. His face hit against the pavement.

"Oh, God! Richard!" René bent down and placed his hand on Richard's back. He helped him sit up. Richard's nose and forehead were bloodied, but he barely noticed them. He felt as though an iron stake had pierced his lower back.

"Fuckin' redneck cowards," René said. "Threw a full bottle of beer." He pointed at the shattered glass and foamy liquid on the pavement. "You okay?"

Richard did not view this as some random act, but as yet another warning to seek distant harbor from the world around him—it was a hostile place with people who would cause him harm.

In spite of this inauspicious beginning, he liked René and agreed to see him again. It turned out that René's mother was a minor local celebrity. Bonita O'Malley Kilpatrick was a stunningly attractive redhead who had been the youngest contestant ever crowned Miss Coastal Mississippi. She owned an uptown beauty salon famous for being a frequent stop for many of the middle-aged, middle-class ladies in town. Located in a bright yellow converted shotgun-style house, with a large lipstick-red neon sign hanging in its front window, Bonita's Beauty Box salon was a neighborhood landmark. René had grown up running around in it, the darling of his mother's customers and employees.

Over time, Richard and René became close friends and saw a lot of each other. But one evening, several years later, the two returned from a movie to find fire engines and police cars parked in front of Richard's house, their red and blue lights flashing. Neighbors had clumped into small groups, huddling close, with fingers pointing. Richard's mother had been drinking and, in her oblivion, set a sofa cushion on fire while smoking. She'd have burned the house to the ground if it hadn't been for a loud smoke alarm and the quick response of a neighbor. That excursion marked the last evening Richard left his mother alone for any length of time. She had become a danger to herself and could no longer be trusted on her own. And, although he knew his mother's accident was not René's fault, Richard was superstitious enough to associate that fateful night with being in his company, which caused him to back away from seeing René again.

Richard awoke, his lower back muscles seized and his torn hands throbbing. A wicked headache bore through his skull, originating behind his left eye. He lay motionless, wanting to drift into the ether again, but continuing to surface, gradually becoming more aware of where he was, and why—remembering how he'd carried Doreen through the floodwater to his house, holding onto her with his shredded hands, recalling that they had taken refuge together in the blistering heat of his attic.

The late afternoon light filtering into the attic had a golden cast. Doreen sang softly to herself as she reached out and touched his forehead, her hand soothing. Without his glasses, she appeared a blur. He pushed against the floor, attempting to right himself. Darts of fiery pain shot from his hands, up his arms, and into his neck and ears. He yelped. Doreen reached forward to support him. She picked up his eyeglasses and placed them on his nose; then she held the jar of water she'd opened earlier and put it to his lips.

Dazed, Richard drained it and then tapped his thick eyeglasses into place. "Do you see my cigarettes anywhere?"

Doreen lit a cigarette and handed it to him.

He inhaled deeply. "Thanks." He offered her one.

"I don't smoke," she said. "Curtis's father did, and I used to light them for him."

He sighed, expelling a swirling trail of silvery-blue. "Was I out long?"

Doreen wiggled her wrist to show that she wasn't wearing a watch. "Seemed like forever. You groaned a lot."

"Nightmares," he said as he attempted to stretch his arms over his head.

"There are nightmares worse than this?" She gestured with her hands at their surroundings.

Richard hunched his shoulders and shortened his neck. "Damn back's been a curse since I was twenty." It had been damaged the night he'd been hit by that beer bottle. He tried to straighten himself but felt as if every joint in his body had rusted. *Oil can,* he thought. Rivulets of sweat dribbled down his forehead and off the end of his nose. His eyelids twitched.

Doreen popped open a can of Diet Coke for each of them. They both drank. She finished hers first, trying to disguise her belches as she made her way to the louvered vent. She wedged a couple fingers between its fixed slats, wanting to force them open. "Ooowee! Wouldn't it be nice to get some air in here and see what's happenin' out there?" She picked up a piece of cardboard from the floor and began to fan her glistening cinnamon-colored face.

Richard struggled to a standing position, an audible groan accompanying his movements. The low ceiling forced him to bend forward, his demeanor cautious and deliberate, his skin color slightly green. "Get out the way," he said as he avoided the dog stretched out on the floor and continued toward the vent.

Doreen squinted. "Where do you want me to go?"

"Anywhere else," he said. "I'm going to give you some air and a view."

Richard inched his way closer to the vent and strained to bend down on to one knee. From there, he turned and lowered himself onto his bottom. With Doreen's assistance, he lay back, propped up on his elbows. A sour taste filled his mouth. He could hardly hold his tremulous legs in the air long enough to take a breath, much less kick. When he did kick, nothing happened. "Your turn," he said.

"It's okay for me to bust them out?" she asked as she exchanged places with him. "Because I will," she said, speaking forcefully. "I can."

"Fine. I'll add them to my list of much needed home repairs." His soft laughter shifted to a rolling resonant cough.

Doreen shut her eyes, took a big breath, and yelled, "Aaaeeeahhh!" driving both her feet against the louvers. The louvers cracked but did not give way. She kept kicking until the wooden slats finally splintered and broke loose, most of them flying out of the framing. She pulled the remaining fragments away with her hands, ripping open a hole large enough to crawl through.

Soft evening light filled the attic as the view stretched out before them. Richard had to remind himself to breathe. *Water, water, everywhere.* Impossible to believe, and yet there it was—a scene drenched in the reflected orange, pink, and violet hues of an ironically stunning sunset with the top thirds of neighboring houses emerging from the dark invading water like islands. The shimmering of water stretched in every direction, as far as they both could see.

Doreen's face slackened. "Holy shit. You were right. It *is* the whole city!" She groaned and placed her forehead against Richard's shoulder, shielding her eyes. Reflexively, she reached around and clutched hold of him as she sobbed, almost pulling him over.

He wanted to say something encouraging and give her hope but, like rummaging inside empty pockets for change already spent, he had nothing to offer.

The very last remains of daylight illuminated a fading lavender-and-pink streaked sky. Doreen imagined all that lurked beneath the pretty pastel veneer of the water below: snakes, rats, dead people. Too awful. She turned her attention to the large yellow dog spread over the attic floor like softened butter. It seemed impossible that circumstances could have changed so quickly and so drastically since she and Markita had driven to a suburban house in Metairie, to the home of the pink complected man with a nose like a reddish pickle who wanted to sell his dog. She pictured the expression on the man's face, how he'd appeared more irritated than pleased to find two black women ringing his doorbell, and to learn that they had been the people who'd called earlier and asked about the yellow Labrador retriever he'd advertised in the newspaper. How hesitant he had been to allow them into his house.

"It's been five days. You're the only ones who answered our ad," the man said, shaking his head as he led the women into his den. A heavy-set dog got to his feet and stared at the two women. "This is Buddy," the man said. Doreen reached forward to pat the top of the dog's head, but he backed away. "Try holdin' your hand out, palm up and stayin' still," the owner suggested. "Let him come to you." While he spoke to Doreen, the man's eyes remained glued on Markita, who strolled around, inspecting his extensive display of bowling trophies.

"Very impressive," Markita said when she noticed how closely the man watched her. "You must be pretty darn good to win all these." Her fingers reached out as if in slow motion, stopping just shy of the largest trophy in the room.

Wisps of mousey brown hair stood up like antennae on the man's glossy pink scalp. "Please don't touch 'em," he told her. "They're not all mine. The wife bowls, too."

Markita's hand hovered before a three-foot high trophy topped with a sculpture of a couple bowling in tandem. "Yes, indeedy," she said, leaning forward to read the inscription. "Some kind of seriously good."

The man's wife, a skinny wizened thing, watched them from the kitchen, coughing and clearing her throat. After the two women had been in her house for a few minutes, she began to shuffle between the kitchen and the den, hacking and tapping on the crystal of her watch with her fingernail. "Get on with it," she told her husband. "Remember, we have that appointment."

"What appointment?" he asked and then said, "Oh, yeah, that appointment."

During their exchange, the dog moseyed over to Doreen, and leaned against her. He looked up at her, his wagging tail slapping against her leg. "Why are you selling him?" Doreen asked, smiling as she petted the dog.

"No choice," the man replied. "Our granddaughter's come down with asthma." He pulled a handkerchief from his pocket, wiped his brow, and blew his nose.

"I want a dog as a present for my son," she told him. "He's going to be eleven. I've never owned a dog before, so I thought I'd get an older one—one that was already trained."

"Buddy's a great dog, patient and housebroken," the man replied. "He's gentle. And very good with kids." The man's eyes glistened as he stroked the dog's broad back.

Markita and Doreen exchanged nods and smiles. "How old is he?" Doreen asked.

"He'll be seven in a few weeks. I'll get you his papers. You'll need to take him to a vet once a year. Keep up on his shots. And be sure to feed him high-quality food. None of that crappy store-brand stuff. This here's a pedigreed dog. He's registered."

"Tell 'em we'll only take cash," his wife called out hoarsely, having returned to her perch in the kitchen.

"Lucky thing!" Markita crowed in response. "We only brought cash."

Doreen counted out seventy-five dollars and handed it to the man. He recounted it before going to the kitchen and turning the bills over to his wife.

"I thought they was wasting our time," the man's wife said loud enough to be overheard as he gave her the money. "I always thought those people was scared a dogs."

"Those people," Markita mouthed to Doreen.

"Please give him a good home," the man said as he handed Doreen an envelope with papers and medical records. "He's been such a good dog." The man fastened a leash to the collar around the dog's neck and handed Markita a small bag of dry dog food.

Markita flashed a broad, toothy grin. "Please tell your wife that *we people*—and I'm going to presume she meant school-teachers—aren't afraid of dogs one bit. We love them, don't we, Doreen?"

"We do," was about all the sarcasm Doreen wished to muster.

The man's face flushed redder as he gestured with an open hand toward the front door and showed them the way out. "Please give him a good home," he repeated, his eyes filling with tears.

"I will," Doreen replied with sincerity before leading the dog from the house to Markita's car. The dog jumped onto the car's backseat without hesitation. He laid down as Doreen got into the front.

Markita sat completely still for a moment and then exploded into laughter. "Damn bowlers," she said as she started the car, slapping the steering wheel several times and continuing to giggle.

Doreen laughed, too. Laughter felt good after that transaction.

It was on their drive back into town, while bringing Buddy to her house, that Doreen first saw some folks preparing for Katrina's arrival. Though the storm had only just cut across southern Florida and entered the Gulf, and no one had any idea where it would go next—the best estimate being Alabama as the most likely target—she and Markita saw several houses with sheets of plywood nailed over their windows.

"Talk to me," she urged. "Please," she added when he didn't respond.

Richard blew cigarette smoke into the darkness and sighed. "About what?"

"Anything. I don't care. I'm about to go crazy." She issued a brittle laugh. "Tell me what you used to do before you started caring for your mother."

"Why would you want to know something like that?"

"Because I'm curious, and interested."

"I was in school—studying acting," he told her.

"I had no idea. See. That *is* interesting. Where did you study?"

"New York City. I was taking classes from Uta Hagen at the Actors Studio."

Doreen had no idea who Uta Hagen might be, or anything about the Actors Studio, but was thrilled to engage Richard in an actual conversation. The night had grown black and silent, and there would be so many hours to fill. "Were you in any plays or movies? Anything I might have seen or heard of?"

"Never got the chance." He sounded embarrassed as well as regretful. "My father died at the end of my first semester, so I came back to New Orleans to care for my mother. She'd started to drink and needed my help. I had always intended to go back to New York someday, but then she came down with Alzheimer's."

"How did you get interested in acting? High school plays?"

"Oh no, not in high school. I was way too shy."

"Why acting, then?"

"You know how children are when they're pretending?" Richard asked. "How absorbed they can become in whatever they're imagining?"

She hummed yes, that she did. "I am a fourth-grade teacher, don't forget."

"Well, I found out that I liked pretending to be someone else more than being myself. When I was acting, I could be anybody, do anything. I probably would have enjoyed high school a whole lot better if I had started acting back then."

"How did you wind up in New York City?"

"Auditioned," he replied. "Did it on a lark. I've always loved movies. Read a notice in *The Times-Picayune* that they'd be doing auditions at the little theatre in the Quarter. Surprised myself when I went there, totally on a whim."

"You must have a lot of talent."

"Don't know about that. But I did enjoy it."

She thought a moment. "Were you in any operas?"

"Operas? Lord, no. I can't sing like that. Opera requires years of voice training. Why? Why would you ask about operas?"

Doreen took a slow breath. Instinct told her to tread carefully and not to pry much further. "Because I know you like them, that's all. I hear you playing them."

Richard flicked his cigarette butt outside into the darkness. "What about you? Do you like them?"

"I don't know enough about them to answer that question." She pushed her fingers through her tangled hair. "I've never heard more than one or two, and none from start to finish. To be honest, I don't think I understand them."

"Because they're in another language?"

"That, and because I didn't find them believable. The one I remember—I don't even know its name—begins with a mother getting so worked up that she throws her baby into a bonfire." Doreen grimaced. "Now, I've got a damn good imagination, but once I saw that, it was over. How could anyone believe that?"

"You're thinking about it in the wrong way. Operas are more like dreams than real life. It's their emotions that are real, not their stories so much. The stories are simply vehicles for . . ." Richard tried to clear his throat and began to cough. She patted him on the back. He shook his head as he struggled to regulate his breathing.

"Maybe you should see a doctor when we get out of here," she told him. "It's probably nothing more than a smoker's cough, but it wouldn't hurt to get checked. They're able to treat all kinds of lung problems these days."

Richard shook his head as he continued coughing. He spit through the opening in the wall. "Treatment's the last thing I'd want."

"You don't mean that."

"Oh, yes I do."

She waited for the awkwardness of that moment to pass. "What possible emotion could justify throwing your own baby into a fire?" Doreen wanted to shift the subject.

"It's called *Il Trovatore*."

"What is?"

"The name of that opera. If you heard it again, got past that first scene, I think you'd like the music. It's very tuneful. You can hum lots of it."

"That may be, but no way could I ever get past the throwing-your-own-baby-into-a-fire thing!" She hissed through her teeth as her hand found another small jar of water. She opened it and took a modest drink. She offered some to Richard, but he declined.

"The gypsy woman who throws her baby into a fire has mistaken her own child for the child of the man who killed her mother. Get it? The emotion portrayed is revenge—and how it doesn't work. I know operas can seem overblown or unbelievable, but that's just their way of presenting strong emotions. And that's even more true about the singing. Operatic voices can convey emotions so purely and deeply—feelings like heartbreak, or love, or anger, or betrayal, or revenge—that *you* actually experience it, too, along with the characters when you listen."

"If this were an opera, just imagine what we'd be singing," she said, pleased that this was the first actual conversation that she and Richard had ever had. "You make operas sound a lot more interesting than I thought."

"They're incredible. Each creates its own world. And each has provided a world of escape for me. Being alone all the time, opera is the only thing that's kept me going since Mother died."

"Sounds like I should give them another chance. Maybe you'll play a couple of your favorites for me someday, and we could talk about them."

He sighed. "Doubt that will happen," he said, quietly. "All my stereo equipment and records are ruined."

"Tell you what. When we get out of here, I'll get a record player. Then you can start by playing the records you saved from down below." Doreen pointed. "The ones with that lady—Maria somebody. After that, I'll buy one album a month and we can listen to them together. You can recommend which ones to get and teach me about them. Okay?"

Richard agreed, wondering if she truly meant it. "But only if you'll teach me how to make your shrimp stew. Yours was the best I've ever tasted—even better than my grandmother's—and that's saying a lot."

"Deal." Doreen said, feeling great satisfaction.

Richard said nothing more but seemed pleased. A short time later, he fell asleep. Doreen gently placed her hand on his forehead; he felt quite feverish and his skin clammy. She didn't know if the cause was an actual high fever or the intense heat in the attic. He mumbled and moaned several times without waking, snoring deep in his throat. Using a small amount of their precious drinking water, she dampened the hem of her blouse and dabbed it on Richard's forehead and chapped lips. She was frugal; she knew she'd have to ration. Only two small jars of water remained.

She dozed, awakening to the sound of yelling in the distance. She listened, hoping to hear it again, but didn't. Might it have been rescuers, or others trapped and in distress? She couldn't tell. It could even have been dogs barking, although Buddy did not react. The only thing she knew for certain was that the world had grown silent once again, and whatever she'd heard had been far away.

To occupy her mind as the night wore on, she shifted her perspective, playing a game her father used to call "Opposites." Her daddy liked to challenge his kids during long drives to see family in Monroe and Shreveport. And though he hadn't finished high school, he valued education, and pushed his children to read and study hard, creating games that required them to think. He never seemed prouder than the day Doreen graduated from college with honors and an advanced teaching degree.

What's the opposite of "disaster?" she asked herself. Doreen pictured Mandeville Street as it had been the day before the storm hit. Modestly sized, well-cared-for homes, with groomed yards of St. Augustine grass and bordered with shrubs and flowers. She understood, however, that simply putting things back the way they were would not constitute the opposite of this disaster. The damage done went deeper and was greater than what could be seen physically.

If disaster is destruction and misery, then Curtis—my creation and joy—would be its opposite, at least for me. She thought of the first time Curtis had been placed in her arms, about the miracle of receiving him, and how his birth had brought an awareness of both purpose and obligation. She remembered sensing that she already knew him. She could still picture his face, his tiny hands and fingernails. Thoughts of Curtis gave her reason and hope.

She awoke in darkness with no idea how much time had passed. What she did know is that living through thirty-six miserably hot New Orleans summers hadn't prepared her for such debilitating heat. Tonight's air was extraordinarily steamy even for here. She lay back on the floor, not far from Richard, and imagined how refreshing a tall cool drink would feel, how it would soothe canker sores developing in her mouth and the rasp in her parched sore throat.

Mugginess had turned her skin moist and tacky, and her neck, underarms, and crotch had started to chafe. Thick hot air caught in her lungs and provoked coughing spells when she took deep breaths. The more she tried to ignore the conditions and suppress what they did to her, the more insistent it all became. Eventually her hacking awakened Richard, sleeping a short distance away. She heard him stir, stretching and groaning in the blackness. "Sorry," she whispered.

He grunted.

"Ouch," she complained. "My lips are splitting. And this plywood doesn't make for the most comfortable bed, does it? Poor thing, you must be incredibly sore."

Richard groaned in agreement.

"You did get some good sleep, though. You were out for quite a while."

"I must have been. It's nearly morning." Richard directed her attention to a thin, amber-colored slice of moon in the sky, a few degrees above the horizon. "Moon's just about to set. Figures it would be a balsamic moon. How fitting!"

A shiver ran up Doreen's spine. Her heart skipped a beat and then pounded with such resonance that it shook her entire body. She'd nearly forgotten. Queasiness accompanied the hollow thuds that resounded throughout her core. "A balsamic moon? There actually is such a thing?"

"Looks lovely, doesn't it? A delicate thin sliver. But watch out. It's the grim reaper's scythe. A balsamic moon brings nothing but sadness and trouble."

Beware the balsamic moon! Mercy's words echoed in her head. "What makes a moon—balsamic? And how often does it happen?"

"It's the last tiny crescent before a new moon. See how smoky colored it is?"

"Is there one every month?"

"I'm not sure how often they appear. All I know is they're considered bad and very powerful."

"And they're bad because . . .?" She immediately regretted asking. What did it matter? She didn't need confirmation of its power. All she need do is look at the world around her.

"It contains Pisces, which brings suffering and loneliness. The hardest of times. It's all about Earthly endings and the completion of karma." Richard shuddered. "And you know what else? Pisces is a water sign. Ironic, huh?" He snickered before lighting a cigarette. The flame illuminated his drained face and lit the area around the two of them for a few seconds as he leaned against the wall. He moaned softly as he exhaled and then said, "I feel awful. Like I've been beaten up."

"You ought to drink some water," Doreen said, reaching out in the darkness and touching him on his shoulder. "You're probably getting dehydrated."

"Not now, thanks."

"How'd you learn about balsamic moons?" she asked. "I'd never heard of them before a few days ago."

"Surprised you've heard of them at all. I read about them in astrology books. Most people never see them. They only show up during the last few minutes before dawn, and they're so low in the sky that they're pretty hard to find."

"Nice to look at . . . but brings only sadness and trouble." Doreen released a sardonic little laugh. "Sounds like a few men I've dated."

The two watched as the balsamic moon vanished, obscured by the horizon. Almost simultaneously the dawning light came up fast, with plenty of heat and what felt like deliberate cruelty.

DAY FIVE

Tuesday, August 30

Doreen had to pee—and perhaps more. She saw no place to do it and no bucket or receptacles to use. She told herself to tighten her muscles and consciously switch gears. Easier said than done. The fullness in her bladder and pressure in her bowels would not yield to distraction. She hadn't gone to the bathroom for nearly a day. She rocked from one foot to the other, turning her body into a metronome, the urgency increasing with every beat.

"Got the heebie-jeebies?" Richard asked.

"It's so damn hot in here. Someone better find us before we melt. Busting a hole in the wall didn't cool things down one bit." Without benefit of even the slightest breeze, the stench coming from below had intensified with each passing hour, adding not only to her distress but to a nauseated stomach.

"You could always go for a dip," he said, pointing below.

The bitter look she shot back was meant to be felt as well as seen.

"Careful," he warned. "Keep moving around like that and you'll bang your head." He cleared his throat loudly. A few minutes later, he said, "I do wish you'd stop your fidgeting. You're beginning to drive me batty."

"I can't help it," she mumbled, covering her mouth with her hands. "I have to go to the bathroom—bad."

Richard closed his eyes, nodded, and sighed. "Of course you do." He tapped his glasses and repositioned them on his nose. "Why didn't you say something?"

She diverted her eyes and turned away. "Just did."

Richard attempted to use his cigarette lighter but couldn't get his swollen fingers to work. "Light this for me, will you? And then hold the flame above your head. I want to look around for . . . ah . . . no, never mind. I've got a better idea. Go over to the hatch and climb down the ladder," he told her. "Then, have at it."

"Have at what?"

"You know. Whatever."

"Inside your house? No! I can't do that! It wouldn't be right."

"It's okay. I'm giving you permission. It's not like the water down there isn't filled with lots worse. It doesn't matter anymore. Nothing does. Just go ahead and do it."

Doreen didn't like hearing the defeat in Richard's voice, but she was only seconds from losing all bladder and bowel control. "For sure?"

"Hurry up," he urged. "Now that you've said something, I've got to go, too."

Doreen put her foot on the first step of the ladder and dropped down cautiously. The mere idea of coming into contact with that icky water, simply touching it with her feet, sickened her further. And she certainly didn't want to expose her privates to the filth. She stepped down onto the second rung, her grip on the rails so tight her fingers ached. When the water reached her knees, she stopped, pulled down her shorts and panties, and braced herself by wrapping both hands around the ladder rails once again. She had to consciously work to make her muscles release. It took a moment. When they finally did, her body exploded with a loose stool. The blasts, unmistakable and rude, went on and on. She closed her eyes and cringed, mortified; she pretended she was elsewhere, somewhere alone, and private.

When finally done, she remained in place, not knowing what to do about having no paper. She used her hand to clean herself as best she could, and then dipped it into the foul water to rinse off. Such an indignity. She wept as she dried her hand on her blouse, and then pulled up her soiled panties and shorts. They were wet and repulsive to put back on, but she had no choice. Unable to look at Richard as she climbed back into the attic, she lowered her head and stood in place, not knowing what to do.

Without exchanging glances, he requested that they change places. She managed to ask him if he needed help with his fly, concerned about his cut hands working the zipper. He grunted and shook his head. He didn't bother to go down the ladder but stood at the hatch, aiming, and waiting to pee. She avoided looking at him, inspecting her shorts, squishing water from them, and trying to arrange her blouse to hide stains.

"Funny," she heard him say. "All this time, and I feel like I have to go, but I can't. I've got nothing."

"You probably sweated out all your water. You haven't had much to drink." He asked her for help to sit after walking back and joining her. "Richard," she said, holding his upper arms and lowering him onto the floor, "I don't know how to thank you. You saved my life. I want you to know how truly grateful I am."

"I didn't *save* your life," he protested. "We're a team. Coming into the attic helped me, too."

She shook her head. "If you hadn't carried me on that bad back of yours, I'm sure I'd have drowned." She touched his stubble-covered cheek with her clean hand and, to her own surprise, leaned forward and kissed him softly.

Richard flinched when her lips met his cheek, as though her kiss hurt him. "You do know that I'm gay, don't you?" he said.

She nodded. "Who cares what kind of hero you get, as long as you get one when you need one?" She felt herself blush. She turned away so that he would not see her face. She thought of Curtis, asking herself if it would be okay were he gay? It did seem a possibility, maybe even likely. *I love my baby, no matter what. I just want him to be happy and fulfilled,* she told herself.

Richard hung his head and began to cry.

She reached forward on impulse, confused and embarrassed, wanting to comfort him, but thinking better about taking it any further. "Don't worry, sugar," she told him. "Houses can be fixed."

Richard's head swayed. "I've made such a mess of life. I always wondered how my story would end. Now I know. With a balsamic moon."

The meaning of Mercy's warnings suddenly crystallized! Much of what the old woman said had referenced Richard! It was *his* sadness that drew Doreen; *his* mother who had been the Empress held most dear. "You're just talking in the moment," she told him. "And Lord knows it's a terrible moment. I'm down, too. But once we're out of here, you'll see . . ."

"Once we get out of here?" he interrupted, his voice thin and cracking. "When is that going to be?" He shook his head. "And what will I see? Where do I go then? Tell me. Who the hell am I without my house, without my music, my things? All I had left were memories, and all my memories were attached to the things that are here. I had nothing else. And now they're all gone."

The hard times do not change. Things do not get better. "Don't worry," she told him, though she, too, worried. "We'll get help. You'll see. Thank God we live in America! Right?

I'll bet the president's got platoons of marines down here already."

Richard sighed deeply. She could hear the congestion in his chest. "Having someplace else to live doesn't solve anything for me," he told her.

Increasing daylight revealed how unwell he truly was. His complexion had drained of its color. His skin had shifted from green to gray. His eyes were black disks set in dark, sunken sockets. She watched him light another cigarette, smoke curlicues rising, the embers' glow further illuminating his waxen face.

The two sat without speaking. Eventually, his rhythmic inhaling and exhaling made her eyes grow heavy. She followed the orange dot on his cigarettes swing up to his lips and down to his side. Hypnotic. Though still morning, the increasing heat and humidity refused to grant her an ounce of strength while draining what little energy she held in reserve. Her eyelids drooped. She yawned repeatedly, overcome by the need to sleep, even as she heard voices calling in the far distance once again. "Rest," Richard whispered. Her eyes closed.

Every joint in his body ached as though he were coming down with a bad flu. Red spots had appeared on his arms and thighs. He stood slowly, struggling to maintain his balance and careful not to wake Doreen. He made his way beyond the hatch to the far attic wall, seeking the one thing he hoped might offer solace and make him feel better.

His hand found it without his having to look—his injured and dulled fingers recognizing it easily. He took a firm hold and brought it onto his lap. Warm to the touch, as though alive, he cradled the rifle that had been hidden up here, supporting it in his arms like an infant. His father had given him the seven-millimeter for his sixteenth birthday. Back then, the ornate design etched into its receiver and the iridescence in the grain of the wood stock had delighted him. He had considered it a work of art. Simply holding it again made him tingle, but no longer because of its beauty.

The rifle had been fired on only one occasion, during a guided hunting trip his father had arranged in the dense swampy woods outside Lafayette. Gil Girard had wanted to toughen his son who was developing an increasingly bookish timidity that Gil thought worrisome. Against his wife's protests, he'd determined to take the boy hunting.

Although Gil hunted regularly himself, rather than go alone with his son or bring him along with his rabble-rousing buddies, he arranged for Denny Boudreaux, a well-known and respected hunting guide, to accompany them.

Richard, his father, and Denny spent their first hours together reviewing firearm safety and practicing the art of marksmanship. Denny set up empty beer cans as targets and then showed Richard how to hold the rifle, aim through its sight, and squeeze the trigger smoothly so that it wouldn't jerk. For the first few shots, Denny held the weapon in tandem with Richard, wrapping his strong arms around the boy from behind, placing one of his hands on Richard's wrist to steady him and the other on his right shoulder to help absorb the jolt of the recoil.

Once Denny let him shoot on his own, Gil inserted himself, hovering behind his son. "Pay attention," he'd admonish. "You've got to aim. Careful now. Concentrate." Every time Richard pointed the rifle Gil would repeat these and other cautions, all of which proved unnecessary. Richard learned quickly, handled the rifle well, and soon hit targets with consistency.

After the lesson the three men drove to a cypress and hardwood forest outside town, and then hiked to the spot where Denny had constructed a blind of branches, sticks, and palm fronds. Denny instructed Richard's father to stay put until they returned, telling Gil that he wanted to take Richard to a different blind several hundred yards deeper into the woods. Gil offered to go along with them, saying that he didn't need to shoot a deer. Denny simply held up his hand and, in his commanding manner, ended the conversation.

Richard followed behind Denny on a narrow mossy path through thick brush. The softness of the ground caused their boots to make squishing noises as mud the color of dark chocolate slid under foot. Richard fixed his eyes on the plaid of the guide's jacket, finding comfort in the rhythmic sway of the faded material, which moved like a pendulum, first left, then right.

When they reached the next blind the two knelt and waited in silence for a buck to cross their path. The space was barely large enough to hold both of them. Being in the tight, fortress-like cubby reminded Richard of games he'd played as a child. Denny told Richard to watch for movement and listen for the rustle of leaves, but being in such close quarters Richard spent much of the time examining Denny's sculpted face. Denny, who was in his late twenties, had penetrating dark eyes, an aquiline nose, and a thick mane of wavy black hair, prematurely graying at the temples. He had smiled whenever he caught the boy's eye.

When a regal-looking eight-pointer finally wandered into range, Denny Boudreaux told Richard to get ready, but not to fire until he gave the signal. The buck ambled close, unaware of their presence, a casual tautness to its movements, pausing to nibble leaves from a vine, and pulling the vine down as he ate. Denny held up his index finger. Richard aimed, his left arm locked and steady, his right hand at the trigger. When the buck came near enough for Richard to hear him breathe and snort, Denny dropped his finger and Richard fired.

The buck fell where it stood. Richard felt the thud of its collapse in his gut. Denny took hold of the boy by the arm and the two advanced slowly toward the animal. It had been a clean kill.

Richard was stunned. The buck appeared even larger when lying on the ground. His first instinct was to reach out to touch the animal's tan hide, to discover whether the fur was soft or bristled. He stared at the buck's wet nose and the one big black eye that he could see and thought the animal beautiful. Then he saw the wound between the buck's shoulder and neck, blood spilling into a crimson pool. He grew wobbly and lightheaded.

Denny took firm hold of Richard's shoulders and held him. "Je comprend, mais non. Don't feel bad. Your deer did not suffer. *Tu fait bon, très bon.*"

Richard let his torn hands rest on the rifle lying across his lap as he recalled the lean strength of Denny's body, and how he had smelled of gunpowder and mothballs. But most of all, he remembered the moment when the attractive guide's reassuring hug had changed to something more. He remembered Denny caressing his hair, and kissing him slowly and gently on the forehead; and how that had made him feel both exhilarated and aroused.

He also remembered how, all too quickly, the embrace had ended. Denny had smiled, nodding in private acknowledgment, and kissed his forehead once again before releasing him. More than forty years later, that special moment remained the most perfect and erotic few seconds of Richard's life. Richard never spoke of the encounter, and he never saw Denny again. But over the years, every once in a while, he would hold the handsome rifle in his lap just to remember.

Richard sat across from his sleeping neighbor, holding the rifle in his hands, and rocking back and forth like a troubled child trying to soothe himself. He continued until the stench of something even more potent than the foul water surrounding them brought him back to his immediate surroundings. The odor burned his nostrils and caught in the back of his throat. Pushing against the inertia from both without and within, he hid the rifle behind a post and stood to investigate.

Buddy had been sick. Puddles of runny diarrhea trailed across the attic floor. Richard tried to scoop them up using the cover of an old *Look* magazine, but his injured hands kept him from doing so effectively. Eventually the vile acrid smell woke Doreen, who groaned with complaint. She covered her mouth and nose with her hand.

"Works better than smelling salts, doesn't it?" Richard said. He pointed to the chewed on, emptied plastic tub. "Seems your dog got into that spoiled spaghetti. I can't blame him for being hungry. I'm just glad we didn't eat any. I've been trying to toss his mess outside, but . . ." He held up his hands. Much of the gauze bandage that remained had disintegrated and hung from his hand in shreds; the rest had fallen off. Both hands were mangled, the right one far worse than the left. It had turned various shades of yellow, purple, and black, and had swollen beyond his wrist, up his forearm.

Doreen finished the clean-up that Richard had started. "Poor fella," she said, stroking the Lab's head. "He's been so good." Buddy lay on the floor without moving. "Did he try to let you know?" she asked.

Richard hunched his shoulders and shook his head. "I wasn't paying attention."

"Nolan was explaining to me that when an older dog gets new owners, both could benefit from a few training sessions together. Maybe I should send Curtis and Buddy across the street for some lessons. He offered to—"

"No!" Richard interrupted, his nostrils flaring. "You don't dare!"

Doreen flinched, fearful of having provoked such a strong reaction. "Why not?"

"Because I'm telling you not to. Don't. Just don't." Emphatic, adamant, his eyes bulged. He drew his mouth into a tight, straight line.

"Are you okay?" she asked. "You're not looking so good."

"No. I feel awful." His mouth curved down, the corners trembling. "Like I've been run over by a truck."

"Try and stay positive. Remember, we're both alive—and that's saying something. We'll get through this, sugar. You haven't lost everything. Take some comfort in knowing that you still have the stuff that's up here." She gestured toward all that was piled around them in the attic.

Richard slumped as he lowered his head. Of all the things in the attic, only his rifle gave him any measure of comfort; life and Katrina had destroyed everything else.

Doreen took hold of her album of photographs and clutched it to her breast. "You've got more than I have, that's for sure," she said, gesturing toward the many things scattered around the floor.

"You've got Curtis."

She paused and smiled. "Yes, indeed I do. Being a mom is about the best thing that ever happened to me." She took a breath and whimpered slightly. "But I'm talking about things, you know, possessions." She pointed to the train set in the opposite corner. "Bet something like that has some pretty happy memories attached to it."

"You'd be surprised," Richard whispered. His thoughts drifted. The train's bright red engine and green caboose had once had the lure of gemstones. Wanting it had been all he could talk about. He'd seen the train advertised in a hobby-ist's magazine at a friend's house. There'd been a picture of a smiling freckle-faced boy with one hand on the control box and the other tipping the brim of the conductor's cap he wore. Richard had repeatedly shown the picture to his parents, promising to be good, to clean his room, to do extra chores if he could only have it for Christmas. He'd prayed for the train set at church every Sunday, clenching his fingers together so tightly they'd turn chalk white. He made the same request in his prayers every night before going to bed. When he discovered the train set waiting for him under the tree Christmas morning, he had nearly exploded, astonished, and overjoyed.

On his first day back at school after the Christmas break, Richard ran up to Father LeBlanc, nearly knocking the old priest over with his exuberance as he described the wonderful gift he'd received, how prayer had worked, how God had granted him a miracle. To his alarm and dismay, Father took hold of him by the ear and pulled him aside, shutting Richard in his office to give him a long lecture about the sins of greed and vanity. He warned him never to bother God again with such inconsequential requests. "God is not there for your amusement. He's not some private candy machine. God is not interested in spoiled little boys like you."

A few weeks later, Nolan Lagusi had shown Richard how interested *he* was in boys like him, and then made Richard swear on his mother's life never to tell a soul about the things that had been done to him. Hurt, ashamed, confused, and recalling the point of Father LeBlanc's lecture—that he was nobody special—and believing that no one would care, Richard told no one about being violated. But his struggles to make sense of what was done to him by his neighbor and parents' good friend took its toll. He stopped playing with the other neighborhood kids and spent much of his time hiding in his bedroom. He often cried, sought refuge in books, was unable to sleep, and rarely left the house. The abuse that began when he was ten years old happened several more times, when he'd been sent to Nolan's house by his unaware parents.

Doreen awoke to a noise she couldn't identify. It began faintly, off in the distance, but quickly grew louder and more ominous. *Fwap, fwap, fwap.* In no time the sound ricocheted throughout their confined space. Doreen hunkered down with a finger in each of her ears, waiting for something horrible to take place. Buddy whimpered and cowered in a corner.

"Get up, get up!" Richard yelled. "It's a helicopter!" He gestured with his arms, waving them up and down, urging her to stand. "Use the blanket! Quick! Let them know that we're trapped in here!"

Doreen gathered the blanket and scrambled to the wall vent. While holding fast to one end, she tossed the blanket outside and started shaking it wildly. Her frantic flapping grew faster and more urgent as the noise became louder still. She looked skyward and saw the helicopter pass directly overhead. "Turn around! We're back here!" She inserted herself sideways, slipping the upper half of her body through the opening, while continuing to throw the blanket around, trying to get the helicopter to notice.

She watched the chopper make a big arcing circle and head back in her direction. "Thank you, Lord Jesus! We're rescued! At last! Over here! Help us!" She shouted with all her strength, aware that she couldn't be heard but unable to contain her exuberance. "Yes! Please! Help us!" Doreen squealed as loudly as she could when the man sitting next to the pilot in the aircraft pointed directly at her. "Yes! Hi! Richard, he sees me! Yes!" she called to the men in the helicopter, while nodding in exaggerated fashion. "Please! Help us!"

The noise from the helicopter was deafening. Both men now pointed at her, shaking their heads. One gave the other a thumbs-up. *Merciful God! What a relief!* She released the blanket and motioned with her hands for the men to come closer. And they did! The helicopter flew so close to the house that she could almost have jumped out and caught hold of it. On the copter's next pass, it circled the rooftop, stopped, and hovered. Doreen raised her arms like a toddler wanting to be carried, waiting for the craft to set down or drop a rope. Instead, the fellow who wasn't piloting, and who had pointed at her, held up a large camera and snapped several pictures. Then he made a few twirling motions with his hand, his index finger now pointing up in the air. At that, the pilot nodded, and the helicopter flew off.

Doreen yelled, stunned. "Wait! No! Don't go!" She watched the helicopter head away. "You saw me, I know you did!" *How could they simply take off like that? What are they thinking? Don't they have families? We've been trapped in here for two whole days, for Christ's sake! What's wrong with them? Why didn't they offer us help? How could they just leave us behind like that?* Doreen turned to Richard, desperate for an explanation. "What happened? Did I do something wrong? Why would they fly away like that?"

Richard appeared ashen, as though he might swoon. "You're sure they saw you?"

"Before the guy signaled like this," she twirled her index finger in the air, "he took my frickin' picture, for God's sake!"

"Sightseers," he muttered. Buddy slowly made his way over to Richard, crouched beside him, and lowered his head onto the floor. Richard steadied himself and then placed one of his wounded hands on the dog's back, offering a reassuring touch.

With her jaw muscles tensed, she poked her head outside again. "That's it! I'm going out there. I'm going to throw that damn blanket around until someone comes to get us. I'll make such a commotion that they'll have to care!"

Richard teetered as he stood. His awkward, unsteady movements alarmed the dog, who backed away. "What can I do?" he asked, as he worked to get upright, and then ducked to avoid hitting his head on a rafter.

"Hand this to me after I get out there." She set the blanket next to him and began squeezing herself through the hole, feet first. Slowly and tentatively, she stretched out her legs and inched herself all the way outside. The roof sloped far more steeply than she'd expected. *Don't look down!* Too late. She already had. She flung her body backwards. Her chest tightened. "Shit, this is such a double-whammy! I'm scared of water *and* heights," she cried.

"Come back inside then," Richard told her. "You can wave the blanket at them from in here."

She shook her head. "I can't sit around in there any longer and do nothing. I can't. I've got to do something—something to get us rescued. If I don't, I'll go crazy!" She scooted her bottom onto the hot gray asbestos roof tiles, squinting in response to the harsh sunlight shining from above and reflecting off the water below. She held a hand over her eyes for shade and looked beyond the ruined homes, utility poles, and sagging utility lines; fixed her sights on the shimmering, watery horizon, reminding herself to think of Curtis, and not allow fear to stop her. Terrified nonetheless, she shifted sideways, away from the busted opening in the attic wall, where she paused, waiting to gain more confidence, and for her breathing to become less shallow and rapid, and her arms and legs to quit shaking from the strain.

"Catch," Richard called out, his toss as weak as his breathy voice. The balled-up blanket landed short of Doreen's reach and slowly fluttered down the roof toward the gutter.

Christ! He's made this even harder! Doreen called upon her resolve, and backed down the roof on all fours, crab-like, the rough tiles scraping the skin on the palms of her hands and their radiant heat singeing them. As she came within reach of the blanket, a tile beneath one hand slid out of place. Her elbow collapsed and her wrist gave way. Terrified, she flipped herself over, smacking down hard on her chin and chest, expelling air from her diaphragm, which locked and refused to expand. For a panicked few moments, she couldn't breathe. The loose tile sailed over the edge and disappeared into the brown water below.

With her hair matted in dampened strings, her eyes narrowed to slits, and her face scrunched into a ball, she scrambled onto her hands and knees, fingernails scraping and clawing at the tiles, and feet pushing and skidding behind her. She fought her way back to Richard and the opening where the vent and its frame had been, shrieking. Richard extended his torn hands to help her, but Doreen dove past him onto the attic floor, her heart pounding wildly. Blood leaked from a cut on the bottom of her chin. She wiped it with her forearm, painting a long red smear on her arm and across her face. Seeing blood increased her agitation. Buddy picked up on it and reacted by rushing over to her, sniffing, and trying to get her attention. She pushed him away.

"You're okay," Richard told her. "It's only a small cut. Calm down."

"But if I'd fallen, I'd have sunk like a rock!" Doreen gulped for air before starting to cry, although too dehydrated to produce tears. "And the damn blanket's still outside on the roof." She moaned despairingly.

Richard pressed his two swollen hands together like paddles and picked up a cream-colored oven mitt lying on the attic floor. He handed it to her and nodded toward her chin. "Hold it against your cut."

She placed it on her chin and rolled her head and neck around slowly. She closed her eyes and worked to deepen her breathing. "Come out there with me," she pleaded. "Don't make me go out on the roof again by myself."

Richard held up his raw hands. Yellow pus and dark maroon beads of blood had dried along the seams of several jagged, angry-looking rips. Both forearms had swollen, like Popeye's. She had intended to find a way to clean and redress his wounds; doing so now would be far too agonizing.

"Lord," she said as she held the oven mitt against her chin. "Are we a pair or what?" She pulled the mitt away. Blood trickled from her chin. She pressed the mitt against the wound more firmly. With her other hand, she petted the dog, sorry that she had pushed him away and wanting to reassure him.

"Don't go back out there on my account." Richard lowered his head and mumbled something else under his breath.

"What would you have me do?" she shot back at him. "Aren't you worried about not having any food or water? Don't you want to get out of here?"

"I'm more than ready for all this to be over," he replied without expression.

"Me, too. That's why I've got to go back out there."

"No. I mean over, over." He ran a black-and-blue finger across his neck.

Doreen squinted at him, incredulous. "Are you cracked? What the hell does that mean?" She dismissed that thought with a wave of her hand. "That's crazy talk."

Richard stared at her for a moment, then shook his head as though awakening from a bad dream. "You're right. Sorry. We do need to get the hell out of here."

Doreen slowly squeezed her body through the opening to again sit on the roof. She took a few courage-gathering breaths, instructed herself to stay calm, and stuck her legs straight in front of her, like a kid sitting on a playground slide.

The roofing burned the back of her legs. With her heart beating faster than a trapped rabbit's, she scooted sideways and down across the tiles, a few at a time, until she was within reach of the blanket. Her energy and confidence surged as she took hold of a frayed edge and pulled it toward her. Once the whole blanket was gathered in her lap, she tied two of its corners around her waist and slowly raised herself onto her hands and knees. She crawled toward the roof's ridge with the blanket trailing behind her like the train of the bridal gown she'd never worn.

"Good for you. You're getting there," Richard called.

Doreen kept her eyes fixed skyward, refusing to turn around or look behind her. "I'd better get there—or else," she called back.

Richard laughed outright.

"Made it!" Doreen yelled with relief as she straddled the round clay tiles at the roof's peak and made a show of flexing a bicep.

"What do you see?" he asked her, his swollen hands shading his eyes.

"Water," she said, her voice dropping a full register. "Nothing but water. It's everywhere." She pushed stinging sweat from her brow with her arm and made herself as comfortable as she could.

Doreen spent the remainder of that afternoon awaiting rescue under an increasingly oppressive sun. When she wasn't scanning the horizon, her eyes fixed on the swamped, modestly sized house next door. She hardly recognized her own home. None of this made sense. Water overtaking everything and ruining it all in less than a day. The sight of it sickened her.

Five years earlier, she and Curtis had stood on the front lawn posing for pictures next to a realty sign that read, *"Sold!"* One of Doreen's favorite photos captured her jumping in midair, as though shot from a cannon, and Curtis flashing a thumbs-up, wearing the amusing grin of a chubby youngster missing a front tooth. But now that photograph, like the entire house itself, simmered in six feet of greasy, stinky, polluted water.

She had been thrilled to buy her house, offering full price to lock the seller into a contract. Markita, who had recently purchased her own home on the same street, one block to the north, happened to see the sign go up the morning it went on the market and had urged Doreen to act quickly. Gentilly homes are desirable. The community is pleasant, integrated, friendly, and solidly middle-class. The crime rate is lower than in most of the city. The houses in Gentilly might not have the quaint charm of those in the uptown, but they were well built and have been well maintained. And its location, northeast of downtown, between the French Quarter and Lake Pontchartrain, is very convenient. She could get most anywhere in the city in twenty minutes or less.

Historically, turnover in Gentilly had been infrequent, and until the 1980s, almost no blacks had lived in the neighborhood. Mortgage brokers, realtors, and homeowners had observed an unwritten, but well enforced, color barrier. Thankfully, such ugliness was no longer an issue. Miss Phyllis, an elderly black woman, shared the house two doors down with her niece, Yolanda, a nurse at Charity Hospital; and Sylvester Combs, an older black man who'd lost a leg serving in Vietnam, lived alone at the end of the block, across the street. Most of the residents in the neighborhood, white or black, knew each other and watched out for their neighbors. Richard Girard had spent his entire life in his house. Fay and Nolan Lagusi, across the street from Richard, were now in their early eighties. They had been there since they were young newlyweds. Seeing all these homes swamped with water distressed her beyond imagining. She intentionally shifted her gaze, searching farther into the distance, but could see nothing beyond vast destruction. Her head spun. Her entire world, indeed, the entire city, gone. All of New Orleans flooded. She could only wonder, and worry, about what had become of her parents and sisters.

Her vigil felt endless until someone's calls for help pierced the unnatural quiet. She spotted a dark-haired man in a torn white tee-shirt waving at her vigorously from several blocks away. She waved back. He wasn't saying hello. The man held a limp infant in his arms and was motioning for drinking water. He continued to call out to her ever more emphatically, as though, perhaps, she hadn't understood the urgency of his plea. She told herself to turn away, that she had no choice but to ignore his cries, to avoid glancing in his direction. She trained her eyes on several helicopters buzzing around some of the taller buildings downtown, though none came close enough for her to signal.

She wanted to scream. She could do nothing for herself, much less for anyone else. If Richard were correct and the entire city had flooded, would there even be a New Orleans anymore? Would all the charm, architecture, and people simply be washed away? Where would the music go? Jazz was born here. As were all kinds of great foods. New Orleans had soul and heart. It had given the country so much of herself. Would she just be allowed to die? Would this be the end of the great city at the mouth of the Mississippi?

And where would all her residents go? Houston? Atlanta? Phoenix? Doreen had once toyed with the idea of living in such places. She'd been recruited for teaching jobs in these cities and others when she graduated from college, but ultimately rejected them and their franchised restaurant, chain store suburban sameness. She'd chosen to remain at home, in troubled New Orleans, where the atmosphere was overripe and luscious, where music filled the streets, and where its distinctively spiced foods had been derived from a unique blend of cultures; where even the houses had history and personality, its people partied together and paraded in costumes, and the romantic sounding whistles of boats cruising the Mississippi River could be heard echoing in the night air.

Doreen placed her head in her hands and shoved her fingers into her ears. *How can I stop that poor man from screaming at me? How do I tell him I have no help to offer?*

Hours spent sitting in the sun had frayed her nerves and sapped her determination. She'd have given anything for a cool pitcher of lemonade and an oversized umbrella for shade. But as uncomfortable as the heat was, it was the endless waiting that truly had her unhinged. *With all these helicopters flying around, why in God's name is it taking so long for someone to get to us? They definitely know that people are out here. They've seen us. They've taken our pictures. Why not at least drop food and water down to us? What's wrong with them? Ignoring us is a death sentence.*

Doreen returned inside the attic dejected, her face badly sunburned and her hair pressed tight against the sides of her head by perspiration. A white crust had gathered at the corners of her mouth. "I am positively fried!" she said, taking the last small jar containing water in her hand. Before drinking, she offered Richard some. He shook his head. "Hope you don't mind," she said. He turned away without responding. She took a small swallow and traced it moving through her depleted body. Doreen screwed the cap back on and put it on the floor. "I'll go back out there in a minute," she said. "I just need a little shade time."

Richard's expression remained distant, aloof. She snorted with exasperation. After broiling on the roof, the least he could have done was make some attempt to encourage her. Her fingers had wrinkled and puckered like prunes, her tongue had thickened, and the walls of her throat were swollen and painfully raw. Swallowing had become quite uncomfortable. She knew that she would have to climb back outside again if she hoped to attract attention, but she didn't want to go. Only her desire to reunite with Curtis was strong enough to overcome her desire for rest and shade.

The dog groaned. She went to him. He panted rapidly, his mouth and nostrils dampening the plywood underneath his head. He rolled onto his side. She placed her hand on his stomach. He felt like a limp rag. His tongue hung to one side. His eyes remained closed, even when she touched him.

She searched the attic, looking for something to protect her head from the brutal sun awaiting her outside and found two headscarves lying in a corner. Attractive in an old-fashioned sort of way, one had a dark blue paisley design and fringed edges; the other was light colored and somewhat sheer, with a pattern of small pink and green rosebuds printed on it. Both looked like something a grandmother might have worn. Thinking that the lighter scarf would deflect more of the sun's heat and burning rays, Doreen picked up that scarf and secured it with a black bobby pin she'd spotted on the floor nearby. "Is it all right if I use this to keep the sun off my head?" she asked Richard, pointing to the scarf.

Stunned, Richard's mouth dropped open. He struggled toward her from across the room and yanked the pinned scarf from her head, pulling hair with it. She cried out. He cursed his injured hands when the bobby pin hit the floor and was lost amidst the shadows and clutter. He screamed something about protecting her from that bobby pin, and never letting it touch his mother's scarf, or her head—all of which she didn't understand. Her eyes doubled in size. Rubbing her head, she stepped backwards, claiming a safe distance, fearful that she had provoked Richard's irrational side—the side Markita had warned her about.

"That was rude!" she admonished, sounding as she might with one of her elementary school students. Hurt and wary, she was afraid to demand respect—but also afraid not to.

"Just 'cause I let you up here doesn't mean you can touch my stuff!"

"I wasn't touching your stuff! I just wanted to borrow a scarf, for God's sake! You do know I've been broiling out there trying to get us rescued, don't you?"

Richard scoffed.

"Well, I'm certainly not sitting out there, exposed like that, for my health!" Doreen swallowed hard, the walls of her throat burning from dryness. Deciding that she did not want to escalate things, she reached out and touched his shoulder. "Listen. We're both understandably irritable. But try not to get physical, okay? You hurt me and scared me. I wasn't going to keep the scarf."

He shrugged and withdrew, like a hurt and angry child. "You don't get it, do you?"

Her eyes narrowed; arms folded across her chest. "Guess I don't. I did apologize, though." She took another step back from him. "What I don't understand is *you*."

Richard refused to make eye contact. "Now you know why I don't let anyone in my house anymore—ever."

At this point, Doreen couldn't have restrained herself if she'd tried. "So you punish yourself for being alone by behaving in ways that drive people even farther away? No wonder you're unhappy. Nolan Lagusi said they've tried plenty of times to help you, but that you always—"

Richard's face flushed far beyond heat induced redness. His eyes nearly popped out of their sockets. "I don't give a flying fuck what Nolan Lagusi says! And you shouldn't, either! I told you not to listen to him, much less trust him. Ever! Nolan Lagusi is an evil man."

She returned his stare in amazement. Time to draw the line. "Evil? Honestly? And why is that, exactly?" She tightened her folded arms and hugged her chest. "Because, frankly, I'd like to know. Why don't you tell me what makes him such a terrible person?"

For a few moments Richard stood motionless, retreating into silence. Then he let loose with a high-pitched squeal, his body crumpling slowly, as if he were imploding. Doreen had no idea whether his cry was one of pain or anguish. When he finally spoke, he stammered, "He stole from me."

"Stole? From you? Nolan doesn't seem like a thief to me. He told me he'd been trying to help you for years. Said he'd even given you that cat of yours. That he'd been worried about you all your life. He sounded like someone who cares about you, not someone who'd steal from you."

"Nolan Lagusi care? About me? That lying sack of shit!" he screamed. "Listen to me. I'm telling you not to trust him. And you shouldn't. You mustn't. I don't give a damn what *he* tells you."

"Okay then, *you* tell me! What did he steal from you that's so damn important? Did *he* take a scarf? Your newspaper? Your parking place? What?"

"Don't." Richard dropped onto his knees and covered his face behind mangled hands. Doreen stood and waited. It took quite a while before he spoke. When he did, it was in hushed tones. "When I was ten, Nolan Lagusi did things to me. Stuff he should never have done—to me, or anyone." The words came slowly; they were labored, and his voice tight and hoarse.

Doreen narrowed her eyes and cocked her head. "Stuff? What kind of stuff?"

"Rude stuff." Richard turned away. "Sexual stuff." He whimpered. "I was just a little kid."

She had expected to hear Richard complain about something totally trivial, inconsequential. She hadn't been prepared for this implication. "Is what you're telling me the truth?"

He nodded and lowered his head.

Doreen clutched her knotting stomach and stared. "Are you sure? I'm asking because *you've* been seen watching the kids around here—from inside your house."

"It's true. I do. I watch over them. I'd never hurt a child. Never. And I'll never let him hurt another one if I can help it. He knows I'd shoot him dead first. I'm obvious about watching the kids on purpose. I *want* Nolan to see me doing it!"

Doreen's mind spun between rage and skepticism, wondering if Richard might have missed a child—Curtis. "What did your parents do when you told them? Why didn't they call the police?" *Nolan better not have done anything to my son!*

"They never knew. No one knew. I never told anyone."

"Never told anyone! Ever? Why not?"

"Nolan threatened me. It was embarrassing and I was ashamed. And afraid. People didn't talk about things like that back then. And by the time I was old enough to figure out that it wasn't my fault, people knew I was gay. Who'd have believed me then?"

His accusation and responses sounded credible. "Being gay has nothing to do with being molested." Her thoughts flashed again to Curtis. "No kid deserves to be violated, or to have his childhood taken away like that. It's just plain wrong. Hell, it's more than wrong. If true, it's criminal!" Doreen's hands shook.

"It's true."

"It had to be horrible living across the street from him for all these years."

"I begged Mother to move away after my father died." He hung his head. "It took me a while to understand why she wouldn't, but I do now. You get set in place. Too many things tie you down."

She raised her fist. "But you must have wanted to—"

"Kill him? Sure. But then I'd have been the bad guy. I'd have been the tortured soul who sought revenge. Revenge backfires. Remember? You wind up throwing your own baby in the fire. *Il Trovatore*."

Though she didn't want to believe what she'd heard, her instinct and experience teaching children informed her that Richard was likely telling the truth. She nodded, sickened, praying that it wasn't so and that she would be reunited with Curtis soon.

Doreen returned to the peak of the roof and sat with her hands clenched into fists. *If that bastard has so much as touched a hair on my boy's head, I'll kill him dead.*

Richard's accusation expanded in its awfulness as she thought about it, making her even more desperate to see her son, and to know that he was okay and unharmed. She was consumed by guilt. A few days after she'd sent Curtis over to help Nolan clean his garage, and he had returned without getting the money he'd earned, Nolan showed up at her door to tell her what a big help the boy had been. He'd also asked if Curtis had mentioned anything about that day or about working with him. That question no longer seemed quite so casual or innocent.

"As a matter a fact, he never said a word," she had replied.

She was about to ask Nolan for the money he'd promised Curtis when Nolan said, "I've started an envelope for Curtis. I put the ten dollars he earned in it and pinned it to the corkboard in our kitchen. Wrote his name on it. Every time he helps me, I'll put more money in it. It'll be like having his very own savings account. He can come over anytime he wants to check and see how much he's made." Even now she could picture the broad, proud grin Nolan had pasted on his face.

She sat on the roof of Richard's house, remembering that she had been grateful to Nolan. She castigated herself, unable to believe how bad a judge of character she'd been. Ultimately, she had misjudged Richard as well. She could only imagine the fury he experienced, and the restraint he'd exercised, being trapped in his home, caring for an elderly mother gripped by advancing dementia while his tormentor strutted around the neighborhood, unrepentant. How unfair, how maddening! Richard's strange, antisocial behaviors, the ones that Markita noted and warned about, made a lot more sense now that she understood his circumstances. She vowed to tell the authorities about Nolan the minute this nightmare ended.

Why has no one come to save us? Has the good Lord himself forsaken us? Mercy had predicted that this ordeal would not end well, that Doreen would be on her own, without protection. *"More loss . . ."* the old woman had said. *"The hard times you experience do not change. Things do not get better. No change of season for you. Une honte. Plus de tristesse. Things are beyond your control. The bad around you will not go away but will grow."* Doreen wept once again without producing tears.

Mercy had aimed her warnings directly at Doreen, and she had been correct to do so. That things were beyond Doreen's control was an understatement. And that the bad was not over, and would not go away, appeared depressingly accurate. Until now, Doreen had managed to avoid thinking of how things might grow even worse, but when she looked at the few swallows of water in the one jar that had any left, and her poor, heat exhausted dog lying motionless in the corner, the imminent danger was becoming harder to ignore.

Where the hell is the army? Why aren't the marines down here? Are we just going to be left to die? This is America, damn it! I'm a taxpayer! My father is a veteran! Is there no compassion? Helicopters are flying all over the place. Why hasn't anyone come to save us? What are they waiting for?

The approaching sunset meant yet another night stranded in the attic, but also that the brutal sun would set—leaving the air steamy, but certainly gentler by contrast. Doreen resigned herself to another night trapped and abandoned. She edged down from the peak of the roof, cautiously ensuring that her every movement incorporated solid footing. At the splintered hole she'd made, she pushed her aching body through the opening and returned inside, muscles achy, her bottom sore from straddling the ridge of the roof, and her neck, back, and shoulders rigid from anxiety and constant tension. The exposed skin on her face, arms, and legs had burned to a crisp. The slightest touch felt as rough as sandpaper.

Nodding at Richard, who watched her enter, she didn't say a word. Buddy lifted his head slightly but offered no greeting. She positioned herself next to the listless dog and fed him their last swipe of peanut butter, rubbing it on his swollen gums. Then she gave him the rest of the water, pouring the little that remained into the palm of her hand so that he could lap it up. *So that's it. All the drinking water is gone. Now, the countdown begins.* When she spotted the vodka bottle, the idea of consuming a liquid, any liquid, became too tempting to resist. She unscrewed the top and took a healthy swig, knowing full well that, rather than hydrating, alcohol robs the body of fluids.

She held out the bottle, gesturing to Richard. She hadn't expected him to want any and, indeed, his first response was to look at her as if she'd gone mad—but then he took the bottle and downed several hefty swallows before returning it to her outstretched hand. He shivered from the alcohol's fiery burn. "If I didn't hurt so much, I'd never so much as consider a sip . . . honestly, I hate the stuff." His head shook. He exhaled like a fire-breathing dragon. "It's so harsh, like medicine. And makes you sloppy and stupid."

"I've never been a big drinker either, but stupid is sounding pretty good to me right now." The two passed the bottle back and forth several times without speaking further. She sensed the alcohol easing her body's rigidity. She reached up and massaged the muscles in her thawing neck and shoulders as her eyes adjusted to the dimming daylight.

When the first few stars punched through the darkening backdrop, she had no trouble coming up with a wish. She would make that same wish repeatedly—on every star as it appeared. She remembered telling Curtis about making wishes on stars. They used to do it together when he was little. She sighed; her exhaustion tinged with poignant resignation.

Doreen sidled closer to Richard, holding the only food they had left to eat, an unopened jar of grape jelly. To release the vacuum seal, she tapped the lid on the floor a few times and twisted off the top. She scooped some with her fingers and then held it out for him to take. He declined. "It's moist, almost like having some water," she told him. He shook his head. She set the jar on the floor, reached for the vodka bottle, and took another swallow. "You're quite a guy, you know that?" Her head swayed somewhat as she patted his brittle frame more forcefully than she'd intended.

"That so?" Richard huffed and then took a few more drags off his cigarette, painting orange lines through the air each time he swung it up and down.

"Wish I liked smoking," she said, her words slurred. "Looks pretty good right now."

"It's bad for your health." He laughed, took another puff, and closed his eyes as he exhaled.

Doreen tried to read Richard's facial expression in the last glimmer of the remaining light. He mumbled and shook his head as though chasing unspeakable thoughts from his mind. "It's okay," she said. "Whatever it is you're thinking, you can tell me."

He exhaled a swirling cloud of smoke and groaned. "There is something I've been wanting to ask you."

Doreen raised her arms as though surrendering. "Ready, aim, fire. Ask away, anything you want."

"Promise not to be offended?"

She nodded.

Richard lowered his eyes. "What made you bring your shrimp stew over to me all of a sudden?"

That was not a question she'd expected. "Thought you would like it, that's all." Even she heard her defensiveness.

"We've lived next door to one another for years and have never exchanged more than a few words. Don't get me wrong. I appreciated it. But what I want to know is why, why did you decide to share food and conversation with me after all this time? I don't get it. What changed?"

She heard his pain. "I noticed that you'd lost weight. I figured you could use a good meal. I didn't mean anything wrong by it. I was just trying to do the good work." She spoke rapidly, ending on a high note in a conscious attempt to sound upbeat. "You know—helping the Lord by helping out a neighbor."

Richard glanced at her and smiled slyly. His face illuminated when he took another drag from the cigarette. "Yes, I see. I was your charity case." His speech, like hers, was slurred by alcohol. "Someone who could make you feel better about yourself."

Doreen's hackles went up. "I was trying to do something nice for you, that's all."

"Okay, but I've been in rough shape for years. Why never before?"

Doreen turned away. "I don't know. I was under the impression that you preferred being left alone."

"*Preferred* being left alone? I doubt that anyone prefers being *left* alone." Richard cleared his throat and flicked his cigarette out through the vent. "You just wind up that way, one loss at a time."

She crossed her arms over her chest and considered what he'd said. "You're right, and I'm sorry." She took another sip from the vodka bottle. "But you need to understand that black folks aren't in the habit of walking up to white folks and asking if they're lonely and want company. It just doesn't happen that way."

"I once heard someone say that it doesn't matter what kind of hero you get, as long as you get one when you need one."

"Touché," she replied.

Richard leaned back against a post. "You know," he said, "there was a time before people got air conditioning when neighbors would drag chairs onto their porches and sit outside. They'd talk back and forth with one another across the way." His tone changed to one more wistful. "Folks got to know each other then. They helped each other out, watched over each other, and each other's children." He rubbed his eyes with the back of his swollen wrists.

"In those days, I wouldn't have been *able* to be your neighbor."

Richard shook his head. "Probably not." He looked at her with earnestness. "I'm glad you're able to be now."

Doreen scooted closer and placed her hand on his shoulder. "Better late than never, huh?" she said. "I'm glad we finally got to know each other. You're a good man. You saved my life. And maybe my son's, too."

The accumulated effects of sun exposure, stress, and alcohol knocked Doreen out. Without word or warning, she laid back on the floor and lost consciousness, whistling softly through her nose as she exhaled. Richard closed his eyes and, in a desperate attempt to rest, tried to synchronize his respiratory rhythms with hers, breathing in and out as she did, hoping to court sleep. He'd grown weak and often felt dizzy. His breathing had become irregular and labored. He hadn't peed in more than a day. His every movement resulted in sharp, stabbing pains, as though his joints contained shards of glass. The skin around his swollen ankles oozed a clear gooey fluid and the dark red spots he'd noticed earlier had spread over large areas on his sides, legs, and arms. They didn't look like a simple heat rash.

Swarms of flying insects arrived with the lessening light, adding to the many other hardships. They attacked the dog's closed eyes and swarmed around Richard's seeping legs, attracted by the ooze, and biting him. *Damn pests*—New Orleans always had more than its fair allotment, only now it seemed that every creepy or predatory bug that hadn't drowned wanted to share their cramped refuge. Flies, gnats, mosquitoes, roaches, palmettos, and several winged things he'd never seen before careened. Some attacked. He did his best to repel them, while fighting the anguish each wave of his hands caused.

Concerned that his thrashing might disturb Doreen, Richard shuffled farther away from where she lay, slowly sliding sideways toward the hatch, where he could gaze down, inside his house. He checked the water level. Darkness made it difficult to tell for certain, but he believed the water hadn't risen any farther. He noted that without a scintilla of relief.

Continuing across the floor, Richard returned to the vent to gaze at the night sky. Stars twinkled. Tens of shooting stars dashed brightly through the immense darkness; brilliant flares that quickly sputtered and trailed off. Satellites traversed the sky in straight lines, appearing as constant light traveling at a steady speed. The red and white blinkers of commercial aircraft flashed against the inky-black backdrop, too. He sat, amazed that after all he'd been put through, he could still experience awe and appreciation for beauty. Nevertheless, he knew better than to draw comfort from any of it. His home had been destroyed and his music silenced. Being in awe of a bunch of stars changed none of that. All that had been lost would still be gone when the sun rose in the morning. Wonderment shouldn't cause him to drop his guard.

False hope could only lead to even greater disappointment; fighting it demanded constant vigilance.

He heard faint cries, like distant memories, resounding in the darkness. He and Doreen were not alone in their misery. Richard drew no comfort from that horrible reality.

Removing his thick eyeglasses, he rubbed the sides of his nose and again listened to Doreen's slow breathing, pleased by the genuine affection he'd come to feel for her. As terrible as this experience had been, developing a relationship with Doreen lifted his spirit. After all these years of being alone and lonely, he'd made a friend—a friend who had called him a hero. It registered. She was both a schoolteacher *and* a mother. Her opinion counted double. He thought how much he would like to introduce Doreen to the opera and share the rewards it had given him with her. Perhaps Curtis would listen with the two of them, although he knew that young people preferred their own music. He certainly had until he'd gotten older.

Poor Curtis. How terrified he must be not knowing if his mother is safe. Not knowing if she's even alive. I wonder what he's heard. What he's been told. I hope the people at the camp are protecting him. Richard identified with Curtis; worrying about a mother had been his life's obsession.

Over time, his throbbing hands, aching back, and the attic's unforgiving floor returned him from thought into his body. He lay on his side and tried to rest. While shifting around in search of the least uncomfortable position, he rolled onto something crunchy and stiff. It was an old straw hat his father had worn when working in the yard. Though it had become too dark to see well, Richard recognized the hat by its shape, broad brim, and feel. Its residual smell of grass and sweat provoked strong memories of his father, who'd worn it when cutting and raking the lawn, and when trimming the persimmon and loquat trees in their backyard.

Richard missed his parents. He even missed being miserable and isolated in his living room, mourning their absence while sitting on his high-backed chair listening to music. Before Katrina, each day had seemed an eternity, something he sought to get through. Now he would have done most anything to reclaim the diminished life he'd known before the storm. He promised that, were it possible to return someday, he would never complain about any of it, ever again.

During the fourteen years his mother had deteriorated with Alzheimer's, he had served as her one-man intensive care unit, doing anything and everything possible to ward off her inevitable demise. Death had been his long-fought foe.

Many of the tools he'd used in combat surrounded him in the attic—plastic sheets, rubber gloves, syringes. He wondered if during his mother's decline, which had been protracted, relentless, and cruel, had she wished for her life to end. Early on, when language began to fail her and fearfulness replaced rationality, she had wandered through the house pleading for Richard to "take her home." He'd tried to reassure her that she was already home, giving her guided tours inside their house and patiently showing her things that should have been familiar. When she persisted, he decided that "take me home" might be his mother's way of asking to be made well again, and for the world around her to make sense. Might she have been saying something entirely different? It occurred to him now that she might have been asking him to let her go—to allow her to die instead. If so, all those years of combating her death had done her a grave disservice.

DAY SIX
Wednesday, August 31

His father's gold watch glinted in the early morning sunlight. Richard picked it up with his injured hands. No simple task. Though painful, his swollen fingers were oddly numb, and fine motor movements beyond difficult. It required several tries, and when he finally held the watch in the palm of his hand, his spirits sank further. Water droplets fogged the inside of the crystal. Katrina had ruined the watch, as she had so many of his other keepsakes.

Richard's father, Gil Girard, had been a big boisterous man with large appetites, very different from his sensitive, introverted son; and yet Gil had made efforts to bridge the widening gap between them. Those attempts ended, however, when Richard confessed to being a homosexual on a trip home from acting school in New York City. Richard had sought acceptance and understanding, but instead received his father's disappointment. Gil became uncomfortable in his presence, and reacted coldly and with distance. His only remark had been, "I beg you not to embarrass us."

Richard had always hoped to make his father proud. Whether he caused his father embarrassment or not, he knew that he had failed him by the foremost standard his father used to measure a man. Richard's mother, by contrast, dealt with the news as she did most things. After reassuring him that she would always love him, she said, "You do know I'll be blamed, don't you? Everyone thinks it's the mother's fault. Dear Lord, why does everything always happen to me?"

About two months after Richard's confession, Gil Girard died of a massive heart attack. The doctor said the cause had been plaque, accumulating over many years, which had broken loose and caused a thrombosis. His father's excessive weight, heavy smoking, elevated blood pressure, and high cholesterol had conspired against him. Richard's mother suggested a different theory—that his father had died of a broken heart. "He so wanted you to be like everyone else," she told him.

Because of his father's death and his mother's instability, Richard felt he had to abandon thoughts of returning to acting school in New York. He traded his newfound independence and purpose to become his mother's constant companion and, eventually, her bedside attendant.

Shortly after his father's death, Richard had stashed away his father's pocket watch—the first of many cherished treasures that would commemorate and memorialize his parents' lives. Now, however, he saw the watch through the prism of Hurricane Katrina. No longer the watch his father had received for his many years of work at the Hibernia Bank, or even the watch he had held onto after his father's death, it was now the watch that had been ruined by Hurricane Katrina. The same would be true of all his possessions—as well as his home and his city. Katrina had left her filthy, destructive mark on everything. She had triumphed.

Daylight reflected off the water outside and shimmered throughout the attic. Woozy and weakened from a lack of food and water, compounded by the previous night's vodka binge, Doreen stretched and moaned. Buddy looked dead. She panicked for a moment, then saw that he was breathing.

Her heart pounded, the beat throbbing behind her eyes as a silent whistle blasted in her head.

"Afternoon," Richard said, shifting his body to face her.

Doreen slowly pushed herself upright. She groaned. The right side of her neck had stiffened badly. She placed her hand on her forehead, pretending to swoon, and said, "Please tell me you brought coffee."

"Sure, and a croissant," Richard replied with a snicker.

Slow and thick, she wasn't so much sick as hungover. She stretched again, hoping to undo the knot in her neck and the pressure inside her skull, which had shifted to her forehead and sinuses. "What I wouldn't do for a toothbrush." She tried to lick her chapped lips and run her dry tongue over her front teeth. It served no purpose. "It's not really afternoon, is it?"

"No," Richard said. "But I have been waiting quite a while for you to wake up."

"Why? What's happened?" A glimmer of hope brightened her dulled spirit.

"I have a gift for you."

Eager for food or drink, she watched Richard slide a tattered-looking straw hat from behind his back toward her, using his elbow. She tried not to let her disappointment show, and again concentrated on sharpening her blurry mind.

When she didn't take the hat, he pushed it closer. "It's for you . . . with my apologies. Please wear it when you go outside."

Doreen's hands went up to her head, smoothing her matted hair and pushing strands off her face. The skin on her burnt and blistered nose and cheeks had tightened and dried. Several sores on her lips had cracked and others were on the verge of tearing open. Hesitantly, she returned his smile.

Richard's expression softened. "Sorry about what I did—and said—last night. It was wrong of me. I'm not used to being with people anymore, much less to being the recipient of their kindness."

Doreen's smile grew larger despite the discomfort it caused. Her fingers moved forward and touched the brim of the hat. "How long has the sun been up?" she asked, pointing outside.

"A couple of hours."

Shaking her head, trying to cut through the foggy residue of the previous night, Doreen swallowed but had no saliva.

"I figured you'd want to get back out on the roof. So go ahead and wear it when you do." Richard said, nodding toward the hat again.

The thought of baking on the roof once again made Doreen want to retreat into her shell, but she placed the hat on her head and smiled, albeit weakly, pushing her hair around to make the hat fit better. "Do I look okay?"

"Better than," Richard replied.

She started to say something but lost her train of thought. *Don't,* she told herself. *This won't help.* A press of emotions surged forward. She began to sob. "Richard, we're going to die in here."

He used his feet to push himself next to her and said, "That's not going to happen. I promise. You won't die in here."

She thought of the promise she'd made so matter-of-factly to her son—to be waiting for him when he got home from camp with his favorite meal, red beans and rice. "I'm scared that I'll never see Curtis again," she said, her chest heaving. She nearly folded in half, her face coming within inches of the floor. When she sat up, she shook her head and made a fist, forcing herself to take several purposeful deep breaths, while working to gather her resolve. As she readied herself to return to the rooftop, she realized that she had begun to menstruate. "Oh, great," she muttered, and closed her eyes. Her hands went to her groin. Mentally retreating, she began to hum and sway.

If Richard noticed, he gave no indication. Moments later, he handed her his last pack of cigarettes and said, "Do me a favor and open this, will you? My hands won't do anything I ask them to."

After pulling the thread and removing the cellophane wrapper, she tapped on the pack until she could pinch a cigarette between her fingers. She pulled one out and lit it. After chasing away the smoke, she put the cigarette between his lips. "I want you to turn around while I go outside again," she said.

Doreen crawled out onto the roof, the sun scorching her already inflamed, burnt skin. Resisting the desire to retreat, and waiting until she gained enough confidence to climb into position at the peak, she looked up at the ridge line and then down at the dark water below, summoning all the courage she could.

"Does the thought of dying scare you as much as it does me?" she called to him.

"Death only scares you because you're young. At your age, it *should* scare you. I'm old."

"You're not that old." She was grateful he'd responded. It offered a distraction.

"I'm old for my age," he answered. "Dying still scares me, but it also intrigues me."

"Intrigues you?" She couldn't fathom. "Not me. Life's a gift God has given us, and I want to care for it and keep it as long as I can." Doreen moved deliberately and with great caution. Before sliding from one tile to the next, she tested to make certain each was secure, wiggling it with her hands before placing her weight on it.

Once settled, she took hold of the frayed cotton blanket she'd left on the roof and tore off several wide strips. She folded and then stuffed them into the crotch of her panties to control her bleeding. *One indignity after another.*

The blanket escaped her hold and fell off the roof. The sun's heat intensified skin irritations that were already itchy. Dried crusts of salt had replaced her sweat and clung to her forehead and the sides of her face. She paused to pick and scratch. Below, a small section of the green tin roofing from the Lagusi's garage floated nearby. *I'm going to live through this, if only to make sure everyone knows what that monster has done.*

Hottest day ever! Positively airless. *It's got to be over 120 degrees!* Doreen resumed her duty as silent sentry, searching the endless stretches of water and roofs concealing the ordinarily familiar landscape surrounding her home. Thirst and hunger, stench and swelter compounded the occasional bouts of vertigo she began to experience. Every so often, the world would whirl and appear to float upwards, causing dizziness and a loss of balance. Determined to remain where rescuers could see her, she leaned back against the roof, securing herself. Being up high while feeling dizzy wasn't a great combination. She shifted her attention to scraping film from her tongue, and digging at her teeth and the inside of her cheeks with her fingernails to remove the acrid coating inside her mouth. Tiring, she dropped back flat, lying against the tiles, and covering her face with the straw hat. Then she closed her eyes, unable to resist rest.

She hadn't known that she'd fallen asleep until the resounding growl of a motor roused her. Rubbing her eyes, she raised her head to scan her devastated neighborhood. She surveyed the horizon, pleased that the vertigo she'd experienced, while not entirely gone, had reduced considerably. The sun had shifted lower in the sky, its light changing from white to golden and casting long shadows. Unable to locate the source of the rumbling noise that awakened her, she stood slowly and incrementally, eager to look around although fearful of falling; trying to keep her balance like a tightrope walker does, with arms held out to her sides.

The motor's noise grew louder and more defined. She saw a shiny metal skiff skirting and bumping over the water. *Oh my God! Someone is coming!* Her hands flew up in the air. "Richard!" She knocked her heel against the roof a couple of times, banging to ensure she had his attention. The small boat bounced on the dark water, glinting in the sunlight. It turned sharply and headed in their direction. She glanced behind her to see if the man who had held up a baby, or any others, might be in sight. Perhaps they had heard the boat, too, but no one appeared. The man with the baby hadn't shown himself since that first time. She could not bear to think what might have become of him and the child. "Richard!" she screamed over the sounds of the boat as it continued in their direction. "Are you looking? Do you see it?" The debris-filled water spread, curled, and splashed against the top halves of houses as the aluminum craft continued toward them.

Richard grimaced as he stuck his head through the attic hole, shielding his eyes with a grotesquely swollen hand, while gesturing modestly with the other. "Hey! Over here! Help!" His voice sounded weak and sickly, and he immediately ducked back inside.

The boat slowed as it approached the house. A fellow holding the tiller waved and then yelled at his passengers to remain seated. No one had so much as raised a finger. They looked incapable of doing so—too wet, too exhausted, and far too stunned.

The boat drifted toward the house. After flipping a fender over the side, a young man raised his head and saluted. "Guidry Hebert, at your service," he shouted to Doreen. "Volunteer in the new Cajun Navy." The young, short, and slender fellow had large brown eyes and a fair complexion. He smiled. Mounds of curly brown hair stuck out from under his reversed baseball cap. "Ain't much room in here." He gestured in the direction of his ten passengers. "But I think we can squeeze one more in."

"There's two of us. And a dog." Doreen pointed down toward the attic below her.

"Oh." The fellow shook his head. "Sorry. I'm pushin' my luck just takin' you." He spoke with a thick Cajun accent. "How 'bout I come back later to get the three of you?"

"No, no! Wait!" she implored. "Richard," she called. "Show yourself. Come out here."

Richard poked his head through the hole. "I'm okay. Take her with you. Please. I'll be fine staying here for a while longer." He spoke in gasps as he looked at Doreen. "Don't worry. I'll take care of Buddy." He strained to be heard over the engine's grumble. "Go on," he told her. "Find your parents and get in touch with Curtis. He must be beside himself."

Doreen's head swiveled; she glanced at Richard and then at Guidry Hebert. "No. You can take both of us. I know you can. I'll sit on the floor. I won't take much room. Honest. I won't!"

The young man shook his head. "Sorry, ma'am, it wouldn't be safe for everybody else. Don't have enough life-jackets as is. Was thinkin' I could take one of you, but maybe it's better for both of you to wait till I can get back."

"No! Go with him, Doreen," Richard urged. "Buddy and I will meet up with you later. Where is it you're going to take her?" he asked.

"To the 610 overpass on-ramp at Elysian Fields. It's above the water. I seen a bunch of people collectin' there. Guessin' they must be pickin' folks up and takin' 'em out from there." The young man bent over and held up a bottle of water. "Here," he said, motioning for Doreen to catch. "Here's something to drink until I get back. Sorry that I ain't got nothin' to give y'all to eat."

The fellow tossed a water bottle. Doreen screeched as she rocked back on her feet. Though the bottle's weight and the awkward gymnastics required to catch it made her frightened, she did manage to do so and stay upright.

"I got another bottle in the boat for you if you're comin' with us," the young guy said. He pointed at Richard. "Give that one to him."

Delirious joy and utter dismay clashed, competing for emotional dominance. "Please take both of us!" she pleaded, clasping her hands together. "This man saved my life!" She turned and spoke directly to Richard. "You should go. Buddy's my responsibility. And you're sick. It's bad. I can tell."

"You heard Mr. Hebert," Richard answered, breathing in short, labored bursts. "I'll be okay. Honest. You go on!" He took a large swallow from the water bottle she'd passed to him. "Go ahead and get in the boat. I'll be fine now that I've got water." He made a show of taking another swig.

Richard turned away, hesitated, and then turned back toward the fellow in the boat. "How about the dog? He's awfully hot. Can she at least take *him* with her?"

"Sorry. No pets on a boat this crowded. I cain't risk it," he answered.

Doreen hesitated. *What a nightmare! I can't leave Richard! It wouldn't be right.* "I'm going to stay until you come back for both of us," she called to the young man.

"You sure?" he shouted.

"Absolutely not!" Richard insisted with more forcefulness behind his voice than she'd heard from him in a while. "Find Curtis and your family. Get on that boat. Go on. Get out of here."

"Come on, ma'am. Time to decide," the captain shouted. "These other folks need to get someplace dry."

She whimpered and cried as she scooted toward the roof's edge. It felt wrong to leave without Richard, but the memory of that helicopter flying away and never returning, leaving them stranded, remained fresh and terrifyingly vivid. She told herself she was doing something bad for good reasons—her son, her parents, and her sisters.

"Hold on a minute," Richard called weakly. "Your picture book. But first, I want to see you in that boat."

Doreen thanked Richard as she scooted toward the roof's edge. She looked down at the fellow who stood in the boat, which rocked on the water five feet below her. "I can't swim," she whispered to him.

"That's okay, ma'am." He smiled reassuringly. "You'll be all right. Just scoot yourself down some and I can help lower you in."

Doreen turned over onto her stomach and inched her way backwards down the roof until her legs dangled out beyond the gutter. Guidry Hebert asked an elderly male passenger to steady the boat by grabbing hold of a downspout, and then took hold of Doreen's ankles. Slowly, he guided her body out, over the roof's edge, and onboard. The acrobatics terrified her, but she'd done it. "Saved," she sighed, shivering from the fear she'd felt.

Richard grinned broadly. "Okay now, wait a second and I'll get your photo album." He held up a swollen, black-and-purple hand. Seeing it made Doreen cringe. Before disappearing inside, he told the captain, "Don't leave! I'll be right back." Richard reappeared with Doreen's leather-bound album tucked under his arm. After squeezing the top half of his body through the opening, he dropped the album onto the roof and squeaked in pain as he gave it a shove, sending it sliding toward the boat.

Doreen clasped her hands together again, this time in prayer, worried that the album would fall into the coffee-colored water, but quickly decided that if it did, then so be it. What was most important now was being safe—the ability to make new memories more essential than preserving old ones. When the album glided right into the young man's arms, she cheered aloud. The guy smiled, prominently displaying a chipped front tooth and a broad look of satisfaction as he placed the album in her waiting hands.

Doreen shouted at Richard as she hugged the album firmly against her chest. "This doesn't seem right. I hate leaving you here alone."

"I'm not alone. I've got Buddy with me. And don't worry, I'll take good care of him. You'll come back for us, right?" he asked. The young guy nodded and gave them a thumbs up. "See. You don't need to fret," Richard told her. "Get in touch with Curtis. He must be worried sick."

"You come find me, Richard Girard!" Doreen called. "You're my hero. You hear me? My hero. And don't you ever forget it!" As she settled down, she fixed his image in her mind. She closed her eyes, exhaustion spreading and overtaking her body. She slumped forward and fell silent.

"I'll come back as soon as I can. Keep a watch for me," Guidry Hebert yelled to Richard.

"Okay," Richard replied in a fading voice. "Now that I've got water, I don't mind having a little time to say goodbye to this place."

The boat shimmied then lurched backward. The young man turned his skiff around. Doreen gasped with surprise and alarm, her hair-trigger nerves jolted by the ever-present fear of drowning. She apologized. No one else had made a sound. No one else seemed to care that she had. People slid over and gave her a bit more space on the seat. She wedged herself in. Guidry Hebert backed the boat away from the house, rotated the throttle, and sent them sputtering forward. She glanced back at Richard's house. She would have liked one more exchange with him. To hug him goodbye. To wave to him, but he had already vanished inside the attic. *It's okay. I'll see him soon. Best not to drag out goodbyes.*

She took another moment to look at her own home, wondering when she would see it again. What must it look like inside? How much damage was done and what possessions, if any, might be salvaged? Now that she knew she would survive and see Curtis, her next thought was how to check on her son's well-being, and to make him feel secure even though his home and things were gone. Exhaustion and dehydration prevented tears; still, she cried on the inside.

The boat motored down her block, slowly passing the inundated houses of neighbors, all of whom she cared about, except for Nolan Lagusi. *He can go to hell, and will!* While she assumed that misery was far from over, a massive weight had been removed from her chest. As they rounded the corner, she took a last glimpse of her inundated neighborhood and spotted the attic hole that appeared like a single black eye in Richard's house. Knowing that she was on her way out of here allowed her to take her first easy breath in a long time, although leaving the man who had saved her life in such desperate circumstances—abandoning her most unlikely hero— seemed terribly wrong, even if justifiably necessary.

Doreen understood that Mercy had been right; her soul had been touched—deeply—by Richard. Learning of his childhood wounds, of the violations he suffered, and the subsequent years of isolation he endured, had given her a whole new level of compassion for him. *Easy to judge a book by its cover,* she thought, *and far too easy to be wrong when you do.* The motor whined a higher pitch as the boat sped up. Doreen trained her sights forward, holding onto the straw hat Richard had given her. She understood the meaning of that gift, that it tapped into his heartache and sentimentality, and she swore that his kindness, generosity, and heroism would not be forgotten.

She turned her face into the wind, narrowed her eyes, and felt her eyelashes flutter, luxuriating in the first bit of coolness she'd experienced in days. She opened her arms and the space between her legs as best she could. She drank from the large bottle of water Guidry Hebert had given her, the muscles in her forehead and around her eyes relaxing for the first time in days. Right away she felt better and stronger, her entire body responding as if a sponge.

The crowded boat skipped over the surface of the water, occasionally smacking down on the chop it created as they headed in the direction of downtown. Spray hit her face and neck. Though dirty, it felt glorious. She got goosebumps as the engine's roar echoed through the surrounding silence. They motored past the top floors of two-story houses and utility poles, zipping along submerged streets that would have been familiar had they not been obscured beneath the dark water. Each time the boat turned, Doreen overcompensated, leaning hard in the opposite direction, pressing her body tightly against the women on either side of her. Other than the old straw hat on her head and a book of photographs chronicling her son's life, she had nothing with her—no purse, no money, no identification. She carried nothing for personal hygiene, nothing for comfort. She had no possessions at all.

Her fellow passengers, mostly older, mostly black, stared blankly, various degrees of shock registering on their faces. Directly across from her, a young white child clung to a woman who looked as if she might be his grandmother. Doreen smiled at him. The boy did not respond. Like his adult counterparts, the child sat in silence, his face drawn, forehead creased, and his eyes vacant and glazed. His expression described the hidden and far more profound dimension of the storm's damage. Doreen understood that some version of that expression would appear on the face of every child in her classroom this fall—if she would have a classroom of children to teach.

The boat traveled on the waterway that a few days ago had been Franklin Avenue, giving her a lingering view of the storefront sign for Bayou Seafood, where she'd purchased shrimp for the stew she'd made Richard, and several pounds of crawfish for a supper she'd shared with Markita and Sam days before that. *Oh, my precious Markita! She needs to know that I'm okay.* Doreen saw that someone had spray painted,

'*Cassetoi* Katrina! Go away!' in red paint on a plywood plank covering the store's mostly submerged front door. Inside, the store had filled with filthy, greasy water. Katrina had defied those words and defiled the store.

The boat continued past the top halves of familiar neighborhood buildings, stores, and landmarks now transformed into strange, waterlogged gravestones. Doreen could do little more than stare with her mouth hanging open, shocked by the extent of the damage. Broken gas lines roiled the blackish-brown swill, making it bubble like it was boiling; she could smell the discharge. Magnificent magnolias and massive live oaks, enormous trees more than one hundred years old, had been reduced to looking like sprawling shrubs, their trunks and lower branches submerged and hidden by the brackish water.

The boat shot across Gentilly Boulevard, slowing as they passed a man's body dressed in dark trousers and a white undershirt floating face down in the water. Bloated, the body rocked among broken chunks of Styrofoam, pieces of debris, and garbage. Doreen wondered if she might have known the man, seen him at the grocery, or at church, or mowing his lawn. The woman sitting beside her reached over and wrapped her fingers around Doreen's upper arm. Doreen turned toward her to say something when the woman shook her head and put an index finger to her lips. She was right, of course. No comforting words could explain away such tragic things or make them any less horrible.

They continued in the direction of downtown, slicing a swath between tall duplex houses that had survived the Civil War only to be invaded by water higher than their raised landings. The boat's wake darkened the peeling paint on their cypress siding. From one of the second-story balconies, a small brown dog barked at them. A desperate cry for help? She thought of Buddy and prayed that he was keeping Richard good company. Thinking of them broke her heart and drained her of the relief she'd felt at having escaped their imprisonment.

The destruction stretched on and on, crushing all hope that the flooding might be contained to one area of the city. Water covered everything, everywhere. *It had to have reached the Superdome.* She sought to reassure herself. *Surely, the city had plans if this were to happen.* She prayed for the safety of her parents and sisters as disbelief and fury built upon one another. Why hadn't she and Richard been rescued days ago? She wanted to protest the injustice of it, but how, and to what end? Anger would not solve anything, answer any questions. Katrina had been merciless in the havoc she wrought, and though now was not the time to become political, she did believe that somewhere down-the-line there should be a reckoning. Nature might have been in control of events, but the government and officials should be held to account for the inadequate planning, protection, and response. Heads should roll for the lack of prompt rescue efforts. She shook her head and tried to focus her energy on Curtis. She missed him so. She needed to keep her wits about her and get in contact with her son.

The concrete on-ramp leading to the I-610 overpass provided a convenient dock, rising from the water to the elevated highway above. As the boat slowed, the stench of sewage and death grew stronger; it made her gag. Doreen let go of the straw hat she wore to cup her hands over her nose and mouth.

Though the boat's bow leveled and traveled at a more comfortable speed, Doreen knew she wouldn't feel safe until standing on solid ground. Up ahead, she saw people milling on the ramp, but saw no shelter of any kind, or a single emergency vehicle. She assumed that they must be on the other side of the highway, hidden by the ramp's sharp rise.

She rejoiced as the boat approached the ramp, her ordeal finally nearing some sort of end. When she turned to look behind her momentarily, a gust of wind caught the brim of the hat Richard had given her and lifted it off her head. She watched it hit the water and begin to sink as it drifted away.

"Okay, *mes amis.* We're here!" Guidry Hebert declared. Unsure what to do, Doreen followed her fellow passengers and started to stand. All that movement caused the boat to rock from side to side. "*Non! Arrêt!* Don't nobody move till I tell you!" the young man insisted. Everyone, including Doreen, froze in place. "Now, slowly, sit back down." All did. "I will point to you when you can get up. You must get off one at a time."

Waiting on the ramp, a shirtless man with skin the color of charcoal and a couple of frightening-looking scars on his cheek caught the rope tossed to him and pulled the boat in. After tying the rope to a metal guardrail, he reached forward and assisted passengers as each stepped off the skiff and onto the roadway. Two heavy gold chains hanging from his neck glinted and swayed as he moved. When the man pointed to Doreen, she rose cautiously, shifting her weight back and forth, working to keep her balance while pressing the photo album against her chest. The fellow on the ramp extended his hands. Residual vertigo made it hard for her to anticipate the boat's rocking motion. Scared that she might fall, Doreen sat down shaking her head, declining to get off, telling him that, for safety's sake, she'd wait and be last.

When everyone else reached the pavement, the dark-skinned man on the dock leaned forward and offered Doreen his arm, allowing her to move more confidently. She scooted across the bench seat to where she could swivel her body and legs, and with the man's help, stepped off. "You okay now?" he asked in a compassionate, even sweet tone. His smile revealed gold-capped front teeth.

"Yes, thank you," she replied. Immediately, she turned and locked her commanding green eyes on the young man in the boat. "You're going back for my neighbor now, is that right?"

"As soon as I can. I've got some other places to check along the way. If I don't get back before sunset, I'll go there first thing tomorrow morning."

"Tomorrow! But, no, you promised! You said you'd go right back!"

"Yes, ma'am. And I will go back. But I cain't run the boat once it gets dark. And I got to check on my own family first."

"Are you telling me that my friend might be stuck in that attic for *another* night!"

"Sorry, ma'am. I've been runnin' all day. I can only do what I can do."

"His name is Richard Girard," she called out, wanting to make her stranded neighbor more real in the young man's thoughts, and his welfare more compelling. "The house is on Mandeville Street about a mile from the lake. He hasn't eaten in a very long time and is injured. He's sick."

"Don't worry, ma'am. I remember exactly. I'll pick up your friend. For sure."

But when? "Oh!" she shouted, raising her arms, waving, and bouncing on the balls of her feet as the boat began to drift backwards. "There was a man with a baby, an infant. I saw them early on and haven't seen them since. Can you check on them, too? They were on the roof of a house a couple blocks to the east, in the direction of the industrial canal."

"Yes, ma'am. I can do that."

Overwhelmed by a mixture of exhaustion and disappointment, she watched as the young man shifted the boat into reverse and backed farther away from where she stood. She fixed her eyes on him as he headed back toward Lake Pontchartrain and her neighborhood, along what used to be Elysian Fields Avenue. Her stamina depleted, she found it difficult to remain standing. She raised her eyes skyward and asked the Lord to keep Richard safe and to give her strength.

The concrete ramp led to the elevated interstate highway. Even empty, walking on a highway ramp felt counterintuitive and dangerous; it made the pit of her stomach tingle. She plodded upward in the shimmering late afternoon sun and heat, threading her way past small groups of downtrodden, miserable, and hungry people. She kept an eye out for an aid worker—someone or anyone official—but only saw others who appeared shaken and less well than she was. She paused occasionally to gaze out over the water and catch her breath. The heat and bad smells stole all the oxygen from the air before it could reach her lungs. And while no longer parched, three days with no more than a few swipes of peanut butter and some grape jelly had left her slow and listless.

Doreen pushed on in search of a comfort station and some way to communicate with her family. However, when she reached the top of the ramp and had a view of the highway, she burst into tears. The road went nowhere. It merely angled back down into the polluted water. She hadn't been brought to a place of comfort and safety; she'd simply been taken from somewhere to nowhere. Worse still, here she would be exposed and vulnerable. Even the air here smelled more acrid. She saw no shelter, no food, no facilities of any kind, and no aid workers—not even shade—just forty or so survivors, stranded and confused like herself, stuck on a cut-off highway ramp that had become an island.

Knowing that the sun would soon set, and that she had no strategy or plan, she grew more apprehensive. By now she understood it unlikely the boat would return tonight, so when she spotted the man with gold chains who had helped her off the boat, she approached him. "Excuse me, is there any food or water here?"

"No, Miss. Not that I've seen," he replied. His soft voice incongruous and contradictory to his rough appearance.

"How long have you been here?"

"All day. Since early this morning."

"And no one's come to help you?"

"Not yet."

"Then why did you stay? Why didn't you ask the man who brought me here to take you someplace else?"

"Where would I go? I can't go back to my place. Whole city's under water."

Doreen rubbed her sweaty, dirty face in exasperation. "Is the man who brought me here the only one coming back and forth to this place, or have there been others?"

"Some Mexican guy in a rowboat pulled me out of my house and brought me here, but he ain't been back since this morning. I just felt like, if they keep bringing enough people here, the authorities gotta come get us sooner or later."

But how much later? Doreen asked herself.

The man smiled. "If you need water, I got a little."

This tough-looking man behaved more politely, and was far more approachable, than his demeanor suggested. *Look beneath the surface,* she reminded herself, and thought again of Richard, and then of Nolan. "Thank you," she replied. "I'm okay for now. You don't happen to have a cell phone, by any chance, do you?"

"Nah. Even if I did, ain't none working. Ain't nothing working. Whole city's drowned."

Doreen thanked the man once again and headed toward the top of the ramp to scout for a place to sit and wait until the young man and his boat returned with Richard and Buddy. No telling when he'd come back, and when she would be able to leave, although she felt certain it would not be before tomorrow morning.

Drop dead quiet—the way death not simply silences but leaves behind negative space and great heaviness. Doreen had gone and Richard found himself alone, but unlike before, eager to leave his home and join her. He peered outside, watching for the young man and his boat. *He'll get here when he gets here,* he reassured himself. *No sense in worrying about it. Relax. Wait.*

He drank from the water bottle left with him, hardly pausing to swallow. His body expressed gratitude by relaxing the cramps in his gut, but it did nothing to ease his unbearable headache or joint pain. His torn and infected hands had long since gone from tingling to numb, his lower legs were swollen and continued to seep fluid, and the mysterious pimple-like red dots now covered large areas of his torso as well.

Buddy sat close, his soft brown eyes following the water bottle as Richard held it up to his mouth. The dog's thick tail swept the floor as he pressed against Richard's leg. He barked several times, deep and loudly. Richard looked for something to hold water and saw a ceramic dish that his parents used to fill with peppermint candies—the hard, individually wrapped kind, with white centers and red and white stripes around the edges. He steadied the candy dish on the floor and poured

water into it as best he could, his hands swollen and uncoop-
erative. Buddy lapped it up vigorously, pushing the bowl
around with his nose even after he'd emptied it. Richard
poured all but the last sip from the bottle into the bowl and
again watched as the dog drank.

Richard swallowed the last of the remaining water and
dropped the plastic bottle on the floor. The bottle rolled until
it came to rest against a small watercolor René Kilpatrick had
painted and given to him a few months after they'd met. René
had matted the painting. Richard had never bothered to frame
it. It sat upside down against a stack of old department store
boxes. Richard wiped layers of accumulated dust from its
protective plastic wrapper using the front of his shirt.

Lively, fluid brushstrokes and vibrant pastel colors described the façade of the French Quarter bar where they'd
first met. Though René had become a commercial artist,
Richard had considered this painting amateurish—inaccurate
in scale, line, and color. Looking at it now, he saw it differ-
ently. What he'd previously assumed was evidence of René's
artistic limitations, he now found exuberantly expressive.
The intertwined couple in the foreground mirrored the sensu-
ous curves of the building's cast-iron balcony railing. The exaggerated heft and romanticized attitude of the architecture,

as depicted, while inexact in appearance and scale, conveyed a definite and alluring sensuality.

Richard sighed and held the painting close. It had been more than a mere present; it had been a declaration of love. *Too late now.* At that moment, he missed René with the regret of a thousand apologies deserved, but never proffered.

Months after his boyhood hunting encounter with Denny Boudreaux, Richard had composed a letter professing his desires and longing to the handsome guide, but he never sent it. How brave René must have been to give him this painting. He'd risked his pride and rejection for a chance at love and connection. *I never had a chance because I never took one.*

While studying the painting, Richard noticed several reddish streaks on his swollen forearms he'd not seen before. When he tried to straighten his aching back, the room spun out from under him. His legs wobbled. His heart thumped against his chest so rapidly he couldn't take in a full breath. As he tried to lower himself onto the attic floor, his knees buckled. Everything went black.

Doreen watched the soft light of dusk grow dimmer while continuing her vigil at the side of the roadway. She bent her scraped and scabby knees to sit on the concrete, dangling her legs over the edge and wrapping her arms around a metal guardrail, finding reassurance in its solidity. She dragged her fingers through the dirt, gravel, and bits of broken glass on the concrete beside her, spelling out C-U-R-T-I-S in gray dust and drawing a heart around it.

What the hell did Nolan Lagusi do to my precious boy in that garage? She had connected the dots and felt sickened. Curtis had returned home that afternoon and shut himself in his bedroom until dinnertime. She hadn't given his brooding behavior notice, assuming he might have been upset that he hadn't been able to do as he pleased that day. Now she feared something else, something very bad, had taken place.

"Ms. Williams?" A faint voice interrupted these thoughts. Doreen glanced from side to side. Seeing nothing, she assumed she'd imagined it. She returned her attention to a partial view of downtown and the Superdome as the sun dropped below the horizon. Her father had said that they were bringing enough insulin for an overnight stay, but this was the beginning of the fourth night since they'd have left home. *With thousands of people in a public facility, they were sure to have aid workers there, tons of food, and medical supplies. It only made sense that there would be doctors on duty.*

A desire to surrender to circumstance periodically sank her spirits as well as her resolve. She contemplated lying back and trying to sleep, but seeing people mill around made her aware of how unprotected and vulnerable to strangers she would be. In spite of her determination to remain watchful, she dozed off, slumping forward, her chin resting on her chest.

"Ms. Williams?"

Doreen felt the lightest tap on her shoulder. She opened her eyes, straining to adjust to a world edging into night. the eerie presence of someone standing very close behind her caused her chest muscles to contract. She pressed her photo album against her body.

"Ms. Williams? Ms. Williams, it's Celia."

Doreen turned around and saw the child. "Celia Barlow?" She thought the voice sounded familiar. "Baby, is that you?"

"Yes, ma'am."

Doreen took a halting breath. "Come around here and sit by me. What are you doing out here?" She patted the concrete.

The young girl, who had graduated from Doreen's fourth-grade class a few months earlier, sat and pressed herself gently against Doreen's side. She said nothing, but Doreen could tell she was crying. "Are you okay, sweetheart?" she asked.

Celia placed her small hand in Doreen's and rested her head against Doreen's upper arm. She continued to cry, softly.

"Are you hurt?"

The girl shook her head.

"Are you here by yourself? Where's your grandma?" She got no response. Doreen put an arm around the child, who felt as fragile as spun glass. "Everything's going to be okay. You're with me now." She pulled Celia closer and rocked, gently and slowly. Then she started to hum "Ah, ah, baby," for the second time in so many years.

DAY SEVEN
Thursday, September 1

"Hey, mista'? It's me, Guidry Hebert. Remember? The Cajun navy. I'm back!" the young man called from outside the house. "You ready to get out a there and go meet up with your lady friend?"

Richard lay in a heap on the attic floor. Soft gurgling sounds escaped from his lips; saliva bubbles collected at the corners of his mouth. Even if he had heard the young fellow calling to him, he would not have had the strength to respond.

Buddy placed his paws on the triangular vent and stuck his head out of the opening.

"There you are," Guidry Hebert said and clapped his hands. "Come here, doggy." The young man whistled, but the dog did not respond. "Hello in there? Your dog is too scared to come out here to me. But I'm sure he would if you did. Why don't you both come and get in da' boat?"

Richard did not stir, his breathing unaltered.

"Hello?" the voice outside called again. "Are you in there? It's me, Guidry Hebert, from yesterday. I'm back to get you out of here." No response came from inside. "Last chance, *mon ami*. I have to go check on other houses. Many people need help. If you're still in there, make some noise. Do something to let me know. Otherwise, I must get going.

Several hours lying on the floor where he'd collapsed, face down, Richard at last awoke. A large contusion had swollen his left eye shut, the surface pain merging with his unrelenting headache. His eyeglasses had gouged a deep divot in the bridge of his nose. To his relief, his glasses hadn't broken; without them, he could barely see more than a few inches beyond his face.

He tried to make sense of his circumstances. *I'm sick. Where am I? What am I doing here?* He struggled to piece things together. *After the hurricane, everything flooded. I brought Doreen to the house. We climbed into the attic to escape the high water. A boat came and she was rescued. The boat hasn't come back for me yet. I don't know how long I've been here. Must be quite a while.*

Richard managed to roll onto his side. The exertion had him panting more rapidly and noisily than Buddy, who lay beside him. As he reached over to touch the dog, Richard saw his hands. The painfully stretched skin made them look like water balloons. They had turned completely black. He propped himself up on his elbows and slid backwards until he could lean against a post. He sat, trying to clear his mind, alternately inspecting his hands, and gazing out through the vent, anticipating the rescue that would take him to safety.

Thank God Doreen left when she did. He missed her company, but knowing that she was safe gave him a measure of comfort. As horrible as the events of the past several days had been, having her company had been like getting rain after years of drought; it nourished his soul, and he craved more. As he sat, waiting for rescue, he encouraged himself by imagining the two of them building a true friendship, listening to operas, and cooking together.

But as the wait grew longer, he began to wonder if the boat would ever return. He had to do something to gain attention. Richard forced himself to stand. He strained, using every bit of his energy. It took quite a lot of effort and time.

Trembling with each small step, he crossed the attic, calling for Buddy to follow. Pain traveled in horizontal bands around his ribcage and vertically, seizing his lower back. His ears rang. Thinking coherently had become nearly impossible. Keeping mind and body together required all his effort. "Come, Buddy. Let people see you on the roof. It might bring us help."

Drawing upon every ounce of his determination, Richard tried to coax the dog through the vent and onto the roof, but when Buddy saw the steepness of the drop, he attempted to scramble backwards. Richard pitched himself forward and shoved the yelping dog outside. Buddy tumbled onto the roof, sending Richard's eyeglasses off the end of his slick, sweaty nose along with him.

The world dissolved into an indiscernible blur—reduced to areas of dark and light. Hyperventilating, weak, and dizzy, his useless hands groped for his glasses but provided no tactile information. He lost his balance and fell backward, hard, his head hitting the splintery, plywood attic floor. He struggled for breath. His heart knocked against the wall of his chest, fluttering rapidly and ineffectively. The ringing in his head grew louder. He lay, unable to move. As darkness came, awareness went. He let go willingly, too exhausted to resist any longer, and eager to replace his harsh reality with dreams of listening to operas in his living room, with Doreen at his side. *We'll start with La Boheme. The music is beautiful, and the story's romantic and touching.* Whenever he awakened, he prayed for rescue and medical attention. He wanted to see Doreen. But as the sun set, his fever increased, accompanied by an awful, agitated buzz originating from his insides and rippling throughout his body. When consciousness slid away, he dreamt of listening to Parsifal and smoking a cigarette; imagined taking a puff and having his spirit float off as the redemption theme played. It would be glorious. But what he wanted most of all, more than that cigarette or even Wagner's music, was an end to all the agony and pain.

"Well done, son," he heard his father say. "You're a hero. You've made your mother and me very proud."

Richard hadn't heard his father's voice for over thirty years. The recognition shocked him; the praise made him smile. *Let go,* he told himself, and he did.

As evening fell, a brown pelican gazed down from its rooftop perch at a raft of dead fish. The bird remained motionless, a safe distance from the occasional human cries coming from houses submerged in the stagnant water, until a large yellow dog, paddling frantically toward a wooden rowboat, caught its attention. The bird cocked its head, ruffled its feathers, and spread its wings. Its webbed feet left the gray roof tiles and flew overhead as a man in the boat pulled Buddy from the foul-smelling water. The pelican did not change course, but merely lifted its breast, adjusted its wing angle, and glided past, in search of a place to roost for the night.

EPILOGUE
Thursday, October 13

Six weeks later, and just two days after the city was officially deemed dry—while the rest of the country debated whether vulnerable New Orleans was worthy of saving, if it held a special place in the nation's cultural heritage—like Venice does for Italy—Doreen simply wanted to be in her home again. She stood on Mandeville Street for the first time since she'd left Richard's attic, staring at the ruined contents of her house and that of her neighbors. All of it spewed across their salt-burned brown lawns.

She kept her distance from a refrigerator-freezer lying on its side; like thousands throughout the city, it was putrid with mold and rotted food, its stench overpowering. The inside of her house—pockmarked throughout with blossoms of black mold and coated with an oily scum—was almost unrecognizable. Every piece of clothing she had owned, all her furniture and bedding, her family photographs, her son's boyhood treasures, even his school report cards, which she had meticulously saved—every material thing they'd had in their lives had been destroyed.

The schools hadn't reopened, and she hadn't received a paycheck. Doreen had no work, no cash, and no access to her bank account. The insurance company had not responded to her inquiries. Nevertheless, she had been told that she could lose her house if she didn't continue making her monthly mortgage payments.

The ride into town felt like going to visit a cherished friend who was critically ill and on life support. She was not prepared. The damage was far more extensive than she'd imagined; 80% of the city had been flooded, many areas completely obliterated or so damaged they appeared beyond repair. Most of the city still had no power. Major intersections were without working traffic lights. There was no public transportation. Fallen trees and debris continued to block many roads. Most of the houses in her neighborhood, including her own, had been deemed uninhabitable. Residents were only now being allowed to return—but just to look and gather salvageable belongings, and only for a limited time during daylight hours.

Doreen sighed before waving at the three figures sitting in Markita's car. Holding a handkerchief over her nose and mouth, she maneuvered through the obstacle course of swollen cabinetry, soggy drywall, and moldering carpets, her eyes fixed on the bright orange "X" spray painted on Richard's front door.

Every house in her once tidy neighborhood bore that same brand—"X"—on their front doors, but the number "1" scrawled in the bottom quadrant on Richard's door was the devastating answer to the question that had haunted her since she'd left him. It meant that one body had been found inside the house. She'd suspected as much but had prayed that she was wrong. Until seeing this, she hoped that he might simply be out of touch. That he might have been rescued and taken some place safe. She hoped the same for Buddy. Finding him had proven impossible. More than half the city's residents remained displaced, scattered across the country, and who knew where pets had been taken. She, Curtis, and Celia had spent three weeks sleeping among strangers on cots in the crowded basement of a church annex in Tyler, Texas, wearing donated clothes, filling out endless government forms, placing frantic phone calls, and searching bulletin boards in vain for recognizable faces.

Tears blurred her vision. She lowered her head, clasped her hands, and asked God to grant Richard rest. *Amen.* "I'm sorry," she whispered. She shook as though palsied. More tragedy, more reproach. There had been so much. She raised her hands in the air and clenched them into fists. If she'd been alone, she would have screamed.

This should never have happened she thought, remembering Richard's words. Neither the storm nor the flooding had killed him, nor had it killed her mother and the more than one thousand other people whose lives had been cut short. It was the heartless incompetence of those in power who knew the levees would eventually fail and had no plans, compounded by those who stood by and did nothing as stranded residents suffered for days without food, water, or medical attention.

Doreen took a step back and looked at the hole she had kicked in the vent of Richard's house. She bent at the knees and sobbed. Curtis flew out of the car and ran to her side. He wrapped his arms around her, hugging her from behind. "Mama! Are you okay?"

She nodded. "I will be, sugar." She stood and wiped her face with her palms. "I'm just sad."

The boy's whole body heaved as he cried, too. "I'm never going to leave you again," he told her.

She looked into his dark eyes and smiled. "Of course you will, and you should. There are so many wonderful adventures ahead of you. Your life is just beginning." She started to wipe his face with her handkerchief, but then handed it to him. "Do me a favor. Wait in the car with Celia for a minute. I want to talk with Auntie Markita. Okay?"

Curtis nodded and gave his mother another heartfelt hug before he left her side.

Markita approached slowly, walked over, and put her arm around Doreen's waist. "You mustn't blame yourself," she said, giving Doreen a couple of reassuring squeezes. "This was not your fault. You did all that you could do."

She shook her head. "I only did what was easy and convenient. Simple gestures that made *me* feel good." She wiped her cheeks and nodded toward Richard's house. "Think about what he did."

Markita began to say something, but Doreen cut her off. "You were wrong about him. And I was, too. He was our neighbor. He needed our help." She pulled in a jagged breath.

Doreen glanced over her shoulder at the Lagusi's house. Markita took her hand, squeezed it and asked, "Did you tell Curtis about Nolan's stroke?"

Doreen nodded. "He knows Nolan will never be coming back."

"Maybe *we* shouldn't come back either," Markita said. "Lots of people aren't. Sam is talking about applying for a job in Houston or Denver."

Doreen walked toward a mountain of destroyed appliances and ruined cabinetry and took hold of a protruding piece of black metal. "Look," she cried, lifting a small cast-iron skillet in the air. "This used to be my mama's. She gave it to me when we moved here." Tears streamed down her face as she turned it over several times, surprised by its condition. Weeks under the water and yet so well-seasoned that there wasn't a spot of rust on it. She looked around and, for the first time, felt her neighborhood familiar—her life somehow reclaimable. "I got a call from Lucretia Galvez yesterday. She's going to start holding classes in her house and wants me to be one of her teachers."

"How's she going to pay you?" Markita asked. "Come with us. We can find good teaching jobs in Houston or Denver."

Doreen shook her head. "That might be easier, but if there's one thing I've learned, it's that easy isn't always best." Doreen held onto Markita's hand. "There are a whole lot of hard decisions ahead. I understand that you and Sam have to do what you have to do. As for us, I've heard that some of the women from church are getting together and cooking food for people who are hungry, and washing clothes for folks. And soon, people are going to start fixing up their houses. I want to be part of all that. I love this city. It's home."

"But where will you live? How are you going to do that?"

Doreen pointed at the Robichaux's house down the block, where a tent had been pitched on the front lawn.

"You're not serious," Markita said.

"I've never been more serious in my life," Doreen replied.

About Atmosphere Press

Atmosphere Press is an independent, full-service publisher for excellent books in all genres and for all audiences. Learn more about what we do at atmospherepress.com.

We encourage you to check out some of Atmosphere's latest releases, which are available at Amazon.com and via order from your local bookstore:

Dancing with David, a novel by Siegfried Johnson

The Friendship Quilts, a novel by June Calender

My Significant Nobody, a novel by Stevie D. Parker

Nine Days, a novel by Judy Lannon

Shining New Testament: The Cloning of Jay Christ, a novel by Cliff Williamson

Shadows of Robyst, a novel by K. E. Maroudas

Home Within a Landscape, a novel by Alexey L. Kovalev

Motherhood, a novel by Siamak Vakili

Death, The Pharmacist, a novel by D. Ike Horst

Mystery of the Lost Years, a novel by Bobby J. Bixler

Bone Deep Bonds, a novel by B. G. Arnold

Terriers in the Jungle, a novel by Georja Umano

Into the Emerald Dream, a novel by Autumn Allen

His Name Was Ellis, a novel by Joseph Libonati

The Cup, a novel by D. P. Hardwick

The Empathy Academy, a novel by Dustin Grinnell

Tholocco's Wake, a novel by W. W. VanOverbeke

Dying to Live, a novel by Barbara Macpherson Reyelts

Looking for Lawson, a novel by Mark Kirby

About the Author

Alan Gartenhaus served as an educator at the New Orleans Museum of Art and Smithsonian Institution, and as a director of Cornish College of the Arts, in Seattle. A recipient of an Alden B. Dow Creativity Fellowship, he created and was the publishing editor of The Docent Educator magazine.

His fiction has appeared in numerous literary journals, including *Broad River Review*, *Entropy Magazine*, *Euphony Journal* (University of Chicago), *Ignatian Literary Magazine* (University of San Francisco), and the *Santa Fe Literary Review*. His non-fiction has been published by Running Press, Smithsonian Press, and Writer's Workshop Review.